THE HEADLESS GHOST

Look for other **Goosebumps** books
by R.L. Stine

Goosebumps®

THE HEADLESS GHOST

R. L. STINE

SCHOLASTIC INC.
New York   Toronto   London   Auckland   Sydney
Mexico City   New Delhi   Hong Kong   Buenos Aires

ISBN 0-439-66987-1

The *Goosebumps* book series created by Parachute Press, Inc.
Published by Scholastic Inc.
SCHOLASTIC, GOOSEBUMPS, and associated logos are trademarks and/or registered trademarks of Scholastic Inc.

12   11   10   9   8   7   6   5   4   5   6   7   8/0

Printed in the U.S.A.   40

Stephanie Alpert and I haunt our neighborhood.

We got the idea last Halloween.

There are a lot of kids in our neighborhood, and we like to haunt them and give them a little scare.

Sometimes we sneak out late at night in masks and stare into kids' windows. Sometimes we leave rubber hands and rubber fingers on windowsills. Sometimes we hide disgusting things in mailboxes.

Sometimes Stephanie and I duck down behind bushes or trees and make the most frightening sounds — animal howls and ghostly moans. Stephanie can do a terrifying werewolf howl. And I can toss back my head and shriek loud enough to shake the leaves on the trees.

We keep almost all the kids on our block pretty frightened.

In the mornings, we catch them peeking out their doors, seeing if it's safe to come out. And at night, most of them are afraid to leave their houses alone.

Stephanie and I are really proud of that.

During the day we are just Stephanie Alpert and Duane Comack, two normal twelve-year-olds. But at night, we become the Twin Terrors of Wheeler Falls.

No one knows. No one.

Look at us, and you see two sixth graders at Wheeler Middle School. Both of us have brown eyes and brown hair. Both of us are tall and thin. Stephanie is a few inches taller because she has higher hair.

Some people see us hanging out together and think we're brother and sister. But we're not. We don't have any brothers and sisters, and we don't mind one bit.

We live across the street from one another. We walk to school together in the morning. We usually trade lunches, even though our parents both pack us peanut-butter-and-jelly sandwiches.

We're normal. Totally normal.

Except for our secret late-night hobby.

How did we become the Twin Terrors? Well, it's sort of a long story. . . .

Last Halloween was a cool, clear night. A full moon floated over the bare trees.

I was standing outside Stephanie's front window in my scary Grim Reaper costume. I stood

2

up on tiptoes, trying to peek inside to check out her costume.

"Hey — beat it, Duane! No looking!" she shouted through the closed window. Then she pulled down the shade.

"I wasn't looking. I was just stretching!" I shouted back.

I was eager to see what Stephanie was going to be. Every Halloween, she comes up with something awesome. The year before, she came waddling out inside a huge ball of green toilet paper. You guessed it. She was an iceberg lettuce.

But this year I thought maybe I had her beat.

I'd worked really hard on my Grim Reaper costume. I wore high platform shoes — so high that I'd tower over Stephanie. My black, hooded cape swung along the ground. I hid my curly brown hair under a tight rubber skullcap. And I smeared my face with sick-looking makeup, the color you see on moldy bread.

My dad didn't want to look at me. He said I turned his stomach.

A success!

I couldn't wait to make Stephanie sick! I banged my Grim Reaper sickle on Stephanie's window. "Hey, Steph — hurry up!" I called. "I'm getting hungry. I want candy!"

I waited and waited. I started pacing back and forth across her front lawn, my long cape sweeping over the grass and dead leaves.

"Hey! Where are you?" I called again.

No Stephanie.

With an impatient groan, I turned back to the house.

And a huge, hairy animal jumped me from behind and chewed off my head.

2

Well, it didn't *really* chew off my head.

But it tried to.

It growled and tried to sink its gleaming fangs into my throat.

I staggered back. The creature looked like an enormous black cat, covered in thick, black bristles. Gobs of yellow goo poured from its hairy ears and black nose. Its long, pointed fangs glowed in the dark.

The creature snarled again and shot out a hairy paw. "Candy . . . give me all your candy!"

"Stephanie —?" I choked out. It *was* Stephanie. Wasn't it?

The creature jabbed its claws into my stomach in reply. That's when I recognized Stephanie's Mickey Mouse watch on its hairy wrist.

"Wow. Stephanie, you look awesome! You really — " I didn't finish. Stephanie ducked behind the hedge and yanked me down beside her.

My knees hit the sidewalk hard. "Ow! Are you crazy?" I shrieked. "What's the big idea?"

A group of little kids in costumes paraded by. Stephanie leapt out of the hedge. "Arrrggghhh!" she growled.

The little kids totally freaked. They turned and started to run. Three of them dropped their trick-or-treat bags. Stephanie scooped up the bags. "Yummmm!"

"Whoa! You really scared them," I said, watching the little kids run up the street. "That was cool."

Stephanie started to laugh. She has a high, silly laugh that always starts me laughing, too. It sounds like a chicken being tickled. "That was kind of fun," she replied. "More fun than trick-or-treating."

So we spent the rest of the night scaring kids.

We didn't get much candy. But we had a great time.

"I wish we could do this every night!" I exclaimed as we walked home.

"We can," Stephanie said, grinning. "It doesn't have to be Halloween to scare kids, Duane. Get my meaning?"

I got her meaning.

She tossed back her bristly head and let out her chicken laugh. And I laughed, too.

And that's how Stephanie and I started haunting our neighborhood. Late at night, the Twin

Terrors strike, up and down our neighborhood. We're *everywhere*!

Well . . . *almost* everywhere.

There's one place in our neighborhood that even Stephanie and I are afraid of.

It's an old stone house on the next block. It's called Hill House. I guess that's because it sits up on a high hill on Hill Street.

I know. I know. A lot of towns have a haunted house.

But Hill House really is haunted.

Stephanie and I know that for sure.

Because that's where we met the Headless Ghost.

3

Hill House is the biggest tourist attraction in Wheeler Falls. Actually, it's the *only* one.

Maybe you've heard of Hill House. It's written up in a lot of books.

Tour guides in creepy black uniforms give the Hill House tour every hour. The guides will act real scary and tell frightening stories about the house. Some of the ghost stories give me cold shivers.

Stephanie and I love to take the tour — especially with Otto. Otto is our favorite guide.

Otto is big and bald and scary-looking. He has tiny black eyes that seem to stare right through you. And he has a booming voice that comes from deep inside his huge chest.

Sometimes when Otto leads us from room to room in the old house, he lowers his voice to a whisper. He talks so low, we can barely hear him. Then his tiny eyes will bulge. He'll point — and *scream*: "There's the ghost! There!"

Stephanie and I always scream.

Even Otto's smile is scary.

Stephanie and I have taken the Hill House tour so often, we could probably be tour guides. We know all the creepy old rooms. All the places where ghosts have been spotted.

Real ghosts!

It's the kind of place we love.

Do you want to know the story of Hill House? Well, here's the story that Otto, Edna, and the other guides tell:

Hill House is two hundred years old. And it's been haunted practically from the day the stones were gathered to build it.

A young sea captain built the house for his new bride. But the day the big house was finished, the captain was called out to sea.

His young wife moved into the huge house all alone. It was cold and dark, and the rooms and hallways seemed to stretch on forever.

For months and months, she stared out of their bedroom window. The window that faced the river. Waiting patiently for the captain's return.

Winter passed. Then spring, then summer.

But he never came back.

The captain was lost at sea.

One year after the sea captain disappeared, a ghost appeared in the halls of Hill House. The ghost of the young sea captain. He had come back from the dead, back to find his wife.

Every night he floated through the long, twisting halls. He carried a lantern and called out his wife's name. "Annabel! Annabel!"

But Annabel never answered.

In her grief, she had fled from the old house. She never wanted to see it again.

Another family had moved in. As the years passed, many people heard the ghost's nightly calls. "Annabel! Annabel!" Through the twisting halls and cold rooms of the house.

"Annabel! Annabel!"

People heard the sad, frightening calls. But no one ever saw the ghost.

Then, one hundred years ago, a family named Craw bought the house. The Craws had a thirteen-year-old boy named Andrew.

Andrew was a nasty, mean-natured boy. He delighted in playing cruel tricks on the servants. He scared them out of their wits.

He once threw a cat out of a window. He was disappointed when it survived.

Even Andrew's own parents couldn't stand to spend time with the mean-tempered boy. He spent his days on his own, exploring the old mansion, looking for trouble he could get into.

One day he discovered a room he had never explored before. He pushed open the heavy wooden door. It let out a loud creak.

Then he stepped inside.

A lantern glowed dimly on a small table. The

boy saw no other furniture in the large room. No one at the table.

"How strange," he thought. "Why should I find a burning lantern in an empty room?"

Andrew approached the lantern. As he leaned down to lower the wick, the ghost appeared.

The sea captain!

Over the years, the ghost had grown into an old and terrifying creature. He had long, white fingernails that curled in spirals. Cracked, black teeth poked out from between swollen, dry lips. And a scraggly white beard hid the ghost's face from view.

The boy stared in horror. "Who — who are you?" he stammered.

The ghost didn't utter a word. He floated in the yellow lantern light, glaring hard at the boy.

"Who are you? What do you want? Why are you here?" the boy demanded.

When the ghost still didn't reply, Andrew turned — and tried to run.

But before he moved two steps, he felt the ghost's cold breath on his neck.

Andrew grabbed for the door. But the old ghost swirled around him, swirled darkly, a swirl of black smoke in the dim yellow light.

"No! Stop!" the boy screamed. "Let me go!"

The ghost's mouth gaped open, revealing a bottomless black hole. Finally, it spoke — in a whisper that sounded like the scratch of dead leaves. "Now that you have seen me, you cannot leave."

"No!" The boy shrieked. "Let me go! Let me go!"

The ghost ignored the boy's cries. He repeated his dry, cold words: "Now that you have seen me, you cannot leave."

The old ghost raised his hands to the boy's head. His icy fingers spread over Andrew's face. The hands tightened. Tightened.

Do you know what happened next?

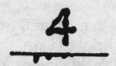

4

The ghost pulled off the boy's head — and hid it somewhere in the house!

After hiding the head, hiding it away in the huge, dark mansion, the ghost of the sea captain let out a final howl that made the heavy stone walls tremble.

The terrifying howl ended with the cry, "Annabel! Annabel!"

Then the old ghost disappeared forever.

But Hill House was not freed from ghosts. A new ghost now haunted the endless, twisting halls.

From then on, Andrew haunted Hill House. Every night the ghost of the poor boy searched the halls and rooms, looking for his missing head.

All through the house, say Otto and the other tour guides, you can hear the footsteps of the Headless Ghost, searching, always searching.

And each room of the house now has a terrifying story of its own.

Are the stories true?

Well, Stephanie and I believe them. That's why we take the tour so often.

We must have explored the old place at least a hundred times.

Hill House is such awesome fun.

At least it *was* fun — until Stephanie had another one of her bright ideas.

After Stephanie's bright idea, Hill House wasn't fun anymore.

Hill House became a truly scary place.

5

The trouble started a few weeks ago when Stephanie suddenly got bored.

It was about ten o'clock at night. We were out haunting the neighborhood. We did our terrifying wolf howl outside Geena Jeffers' window. Then we went next door to Terri Abel's house. We put some chicken bones in her mailbox — just because it's creepy to reach in your mailbox and feel bones.

Then we crept across the street to Ben Fuller's house.

Ben was our last stop for the night. Ben is a kid in our class, and we have a special scare for him.

You see, he's afraid of bugs, which makes him really easy to scare.

Even though it's pretty cold out, he sleeps with his bedroom window open. So Stephanie and I like to step up to his window and toss rubber spiders onto Ben as he sleeps.

The rubber spiders tickle his face. He wakes up. And starts to scream.

Every time.

He always thinks the spiders are real.

He screams and tries to scramble out of bed. He gets all tangled in his covers and *thud*s onto the floor.

Then Stephanie and I congratulate each other on a job well done. And we go home to bed.

But tonight, as we tossed the rubber spiders at Ben's sleeping face, Stephanie turned to me and whispered, "I just had a great idea."

"Huh?" I started to reply. But Ben's scream interrupted me.

We listened to him scream, then *thud* to the floor.

Stephanie and I slapped each other a high five. Then we took off, running across the dark backyards, our sneakers thumping the hard, nearly-frozen ground.

We stopped in front of the split oak tree in my front yard. The tree trunk is completely split in two. But Dad doesn't have the heart to have the tree taken away.

"What is your great idea?" I asked Stephanie breathlessly.

Her dark eyes flashed. "I've been thinking. Every time we go out to haunt the neighborhood, we scare the same old kids. It's starting to get boring."

16

I wasn't bored. But I knew that once Stephanie gets an idea, there's no stopping her. "So, do you want to find some new kids to scare?" I asked.

"No. Not new kids. Something else." She began to walk around the tree. Circling it. "We need a new challenge."

"Like what?" I asked.

"Our scares are all kid stuff," she complained. "We make some spooky sounds, toss a few things inside an open window — and everyone is frightened to death. It's too easy."

"Yeah," I agreed. "But it's funny."

She ignored me. She stuck her head through the split in the tree trunk. "Duane, what's the scariest place in Wheeler Falls?"

That was easy. "Hill House, of course," I answered.

"Right. And what makes it so scary?"

"All the ghost stories. But especially the one about the boy searching for his head."

"Yes!" Stephanie cried. All I could see now was her head, poking through the split oak tree. "The Headless Ghost!" she cried in a deep voice, and let out a long, scary laugh.

"What's your problem?" I demanded. "Are you trying to haunt *me* now?"

Her head seemed to float in the darkness. "We need to haunt Hill House," she declared in a whisper.

17

6

"Excuse me?" I cried. "Stephanie, what are you talking about?"

"We'll take the Hill House tour and sneak off on our own," Stephanie replied thoughtfully.

I shook my head. "Give me a break. Why would we do that?"

Stephanie's face seemed to glow, floating by itself in the tree trunk. "We'll sneak off on our own — to search for the ghost's head."

I stared back at her. "You're kidding, right?"

I walked behind the tree and tugged her away from it. The floating head trick was starting to give me the creeps.

"No, Duane, I'm not kidding," she replied, shoving me away. "We need a challenge. We need something new. Prowling around the neighborhood, terrifying everyone we know — that's just kid stuff. Bor-ring."

"But you don't believe the story about the miss-

18

ing head — do you?" I protested. "It's just a ghost story. We can search and search. But there *is* no head. It's all a story they made up for the tourists."

Stephanie narrowed her eyes at me. "I think you're scared, Duane."

"Huh? Me?" My voice got pretty shrill.

A cloud rolled over the moon, making my front yard even darker. A chill ran down my back. I pulled my jacket around me tighter.

"I'm not afraid to sneak off from the tour and search Hill House on our own," I told Stephanie. "I just think it's a big waste of time."

"Duane, you're shivering," she teased. "Shivering with fright."

"I am not!" I screamed. "Come on. Let's go to Hill House. Right now. I'll show you."

A grin spread over Stephanie's face. She tossed back her head and let out a long howl. A victory howl. "This is going to be the coolest thing the Twin Terrors have ever done!" she cried, slapping me a high five that made my hand sting.

She dragged me up Hill Street. The whole way there, I didn't say one word. Was I afraid?

Maybe a little.

We climbed the steep, weed-choked hill and stood before the front steps of Hill House. The old house looked even bigger at night. Three stories tall. With turrets and balconies and dozens of windows, all dark and shuttered.

All the houses in our neighborhood are brick or clapboard. Hill House is the only one made out of stone slabs. Dark gray slabs.

I always have to hold my breath when I stand close to Hill House. The stone is covered with a blanket of thick green moss. Two hundred years of it. Putrid, moldy moss that doesn't exactly smell like a flower garden.

I peered up. Up at the round turret that stretched to the purple sky. A gargoyle, carved in stone, perched at the very top. It grinned down at us, as if challenging us to go inside.

My knees suddenly felt weak.

The house stood in total darkness, except for a single candle over the front doorway. But the tours were still going on. The last tour left at ten-thirty every night. The guides said the late tours were the best — the best time to see a ghost.

I read the sign etched in stone beside the door. ENTER HILL HOUSE — AND YOUR LIFE WILL BE CHANGED. FOREVER.

I'd read that sign a hundred times. I always thought it was funny — in a corny sort of way.

But tonight it gave me the creeps.

Tonight was going to be different.

"Come on," Stephanie said, pulling me by the hand. "We're just in time for the next tour."

The candle flickered. The heavy wooden door swung open. By itself. I don't know how, but it always does that.

"Well, are you coming or not?" Stephanie demanded, stepping into the dark entryway.

"Coming," I gulped.

7

Otto met us as we stepped inside the door. Otto always reminds me of an enormous dolphin. He has a big, smooth bald head. And he's sort of shaped like a dolphin. He must weigh about three hundred pounds!

Otto was dressed entirely in black, as always. Black shirt. Black pants. Black socks. Black shoes. And gloves — you guessed it — black. It's the uniform that all the tour guides wear.

"Look who's here!" he called. "Stephanie and Duane!" He broke out into a wide grin. His tiny eyes flashed in the candlelight.

"Our favorite guide!" Stephanie greeted him. "Are we in time for the next tour?"

We pushed through the turnstile without paying. We're such regulars at Hill House that they don't even charge us anymore.

"About five minutes, guys," Otto told us. "You two are out late tonight, huh?"

"Yeah . . . well," Stephanie hesitated. "It's

more fun to take the tour at night. Isn't it, Duane?" She jabbed my side.

"You can say that again," I mumbled.

We moved into the front hall with some others who were waiting for the tour to begin. Teenagers mostly, out on dates.

The front hall is bigger than my living room and dining room put together. And except for the winding staircase in the center, it's completely bare. No furniture at all.

Shadows tossed across the floor. I gazed around the room. No electric lights. Small torches were hung from the peeling, cracked walls. The orange torchlight flickered and bent.

In the dancing light, I counted the people around me. Nine of them. Stephanie and I were the only kids.

Otto lighted a lantern and crossed to the front of the hall. He held it up high and cleared his throat.

Stephanie and I grinned at each other. Otto always starts the tour the same way. He thinks the lantern adds atmosphere.

"Ladies and gentlemen," he boomed. "Welcome to Hill House. We hope you will survive your tour tonight." Then he gave a low, evil laugh.

Stephanie and I mouthed Otto's next words along with him:

"In 1795, a prosperous sea captain, William P. Bell, built himself a home on the highest hill in

Wheeler Falls. It was the finest home ever built here at the time — three stories high, nine fireplaces, and over thirty rooms.

"Captain Bell spared no expense. Why? Because he hoped to retire here and finish his days in splendor with his young and beautiful wife. But it was not to be."

Otto cackled, and so did Stephanie and I. We knew every move Otto had.

Otto went on. "Captain Bell died at sea in a terrible shipwreck — before he ever had a chance to live in his beautiful house. His young bride, Annabel, fled the house in horror and sorrow."

Now Otto's voice dropped. "But soon after Annabel left, strange things began to happen in Hill House."

This was Otto's cue to start walking toward the winding stairs. The old, wooden staircase is narrow and creaky. When Otto starts to climb, the stairs groan and grumble beneath him as if in pain.

Keeping silent, we followed Otto up the stairs to the first floor. Stephanie and I love this part, because Otto doesn't say a word the whole time. He just huffs along in the darkness while everyone tries to keep up with him.

He starts talking again when he reaches Captain Bell's bedroom. A big, wood-paneled room with a fireplace and a view of the river.

"Soon after Captain Bell's widow ran away," Otto reported, "people in Wheeler Falls began reporting strange sightings. Sightings of a man who resembled Captain Bell. He was always seen here, standing by his window, holding his lantern aloft."

Otto moved to the window and raised his lantern. "On a windless night, if you listened carefully, you could sometimes hear him calling out her name in a low, mournful voice."

Otto took a deep breath, then called softly: "Annabel. Annabel. Annabel . . ."

Otto swung the lantern back and forth for effect. By now, he had everyone's complete attention.

"But of course, there's more," he whispered.

8

As we followed him through the upstairs rooms, Otto told us how Captain Bell haunted the house for about a hundred years. "People who moved into Hill House tried all kinds of ways to get rid of the ghost. But it was determined to stay."

Then Otto told everyone about the boy finding the ghost and getting his head pulled off. "The ghost of the sea captain vanished. The headless ghost of the boy continued to haunt the house. But that wasn't the end of it."

Into the long, dark hallway now. Torches darting and flickering along the walls. "Tragedy continued to haunt Hill House," Otto continued. "Shortly after young Andrew Craw's death, his twelve-year-old sister Hannah went mad. Let's go to her room next."

He led us down the hall to Hannah's room.

Stephanie loves Hannah's room. Hannah collected porcelain dolls. And she had hundreds of them. All with the same long yellow hair, painted rosy cheeks, and blue-tinted eyelids.

"After her brother was killed, Hannah went crazy," Otto told us all in a hushed voice. "All day long, for eighty years, she sat in her rocking chair over there in the corner. And she played with her dolls. She never left her room. Ever."

He pointed to a worn rocking chair. "Hannah died there. An old lady surrounded by her dolls."

The floorboards creaked under him as Otto crossed the room. Setting the lantern down, he lowered his big body into the rocking chair.

The chair made a cracking sound. I always think Otto is going to crush it! He started to rock. Slowly. The chair groaned with each move. We all watched him in silence.

"Some people swear that poor Hannah is still here," he said softly. "They say they've seen a young girl sitting in this chair, combing a doll's hair."

He rocked slowly, letting the idea sink in. "And then we come to the story of Hannah's mother."

With a grunt, Otto pulled himself to his feet. He grabbed up the lantern and made his way to the top of the long, dark stairway at the end of the hall.

"Soon after her son's tragedy, the mother met her own terrible fate. She was on her way down these stairs one night when she tripped and fell to her death."

Otto gazed down the stairs and shook his head sadly.

He does this every time. As I said, Stephanie and I know his every move.

But we hadn't come here tonight to watch Otto perform. I knew that sooner or later, Stephanie would want to get going. So I started glancing around. To see if it was a good time for us to sneak away from the others.

And that's when I saw the strange kid. Watching us.

I didn't see him when we first came in. In fact, I'm sure he wasn't there when the tour started. I had counted nine people. No kids.

The boy was about our age, with wavy blond hair and pale skin. Very pale skin. He was wearing black jeans and a black turtleneck that made his face look even whiter.

I edged over to Stephanie. She was hanging back from the group.

"You ready?" she whispered.

Otto had started back down the stairs. If we were going to sneak away from the tour, now was the time.

But I could see that weird kid still staring at us.

Staring hard.

He was giving me the creeps.

"We can't go. Someone's watching us," I whispered to Stephanie.

"Who?"

"That weird kid over there." I motioned with my eyes.

He was still staring at us. He didn't even try to be polite and turn away when we caught him.

Why was he watching us like that? What was his *problem*?

Something told me we should wait. Something told me not to hide from the others just yet.

But Stephanie had other ideas. "Forget him," she said. "He's nobody." She grabbed my arm — and tugged. "Let's go!"

We pressed against the cold wall of the hallway and watched the others follow Otto down the stairs.

I held my breath until I heard the last footsteps leave the stairway. We were alone now. Alone in the long, dark hall.

I turned to Stephanie. I could barely see her face. "Now what?" I asked.

9

"Now we do some exploring on our own!" Stephanie declared, rubbing her hands together. "This is so exciting!"

I gazed down the long hallway. I didn't feel real excited. I felt kind of scared.

I heard a low groan from a room across the hall. The ceiling creaked above our heads. The wind rattled the windows in the room we had just come from.

"Steph — are you sure — ?" I started.

But she was already hurrying down the hall, walking on tiptoes to keep the floors from squeaking. "Come on, Duane. Let's search for the ghost's head," she whispered back to me, her dark hair flying behind her. "Who knows? We might find it."

"Yeah. Sure." I rolled my eyes.

I didn't think the chances were too good. How do you find a hundred-year-old head? And what if you *do* find it?

Yuck!

What would it look like? Just a skull?

I followed Stephanie down the hall. But I really didn't want to be there. I like haunting the neighborhood and scaring other people.

I don't like scaring myself!

Stephanie led the way into a bedroom we had seen on other tours. It was called the Green Room. Because the wallpaper was decorated with green vines. Tangle after tangle of green vines. Up and down the walls and across the ceiling, too.

How could anyone sleep in here? I wondered. It was like being trapped in a thick jungle.

We both stopped inside the doorway and stared at the tangles of vines on all sides of us. Stephanie and I call the Green Room by another name. The Scratching Room.

Otto once told us that something terrible happened here sixty years ago. The two guests who stayed in the room woke up with a disgusting purple rash.

The rash started on their hands and arms. It spread to their faces. Then it spread over their entire bodies.

Big purple sores that itched like crazy.

Doctors from all around the world were called to study the rash. They couldn't figure out what it was. And they couldn't figure out how to cure it.

Something in the Green Room caused the rash.

But no one ever figured out what it was.

That's the story Otto and the other guides tell. It might be true. All the weird, scary stories Otto tells might be true. Who knows?

"Come on, Duane!" Stephanie prodded. "Let's look for the head. We don't have much time before Otto sees that we're missing."

She trotted across the room and dove under the bed.

"Steph — please!" I started. I stepped carefully over to the low, wooden dresser in the corner.

"We're not going to find a ghost's head in here. Let's go," I pleaded.

She couldn't hear me. She had climbed under the bed.

"Steph — ?"

After a few seconds, she backed out. As she turned toward me, I saw that her face was bright red.

"Duane!" she cried. "I . . . I . . ."

Her dark eyes bulged. Her mouth dropped open in horror. She grabbed the sides of her face.

"What is it? What's wrong?" I cried, stumbling across the room toward her.

"Ohhh, it itches! It itches so badly!" Stephanie wailed.

I started to cry out. But my voice got caught in my throat.

Stephanie began to rub her face. She frantically rubbed her cheeks, her forehead, her chin.

"Owwww. It itches! It really itches!" She started to scratch her scalp with both hands.

I grabbed her arm and tried to pull her up from the floor. "The rash! Let's get you home!" I cried. "Come on! Your parents will get the doctor! And . . . and . . ."

I stopped when I saw that she was laughing.

I dropped her arm and stepped back.

She stood up, straightening her hair. "Duane, you jerk," she muttered. "Are you going to fall for every dumb joke tonight?"

"No way!" I replied angrily. "I just thought — "

She gave me a shove. "You're too easy to scare. How could you fall for such a stupid joke?"

I shoved her back. "Just don't pull any more dumb jokes, okay?" I snarled. "I mean it, Stephanie. I don't think it's funny. I really don't. I'm not going to fall for any more stupid jokes. So don't even try."

She wasn't listening to me. She was staring over my shoulder. Staring in open-mouthed shock.

"Oh, I d-don't *believe* it!" she stammered. "There it is! There's the head!"

10

I fell for it again.

I couldn't help myself.

I let out a shrill scream.

I spun around so hard, I nearly knocked myself over. I followed Stephanie's finger. I squinted hard in the direction she pointed.

She was pointing to a gray clump of dust.

"Sucker! Sucker!" She slapped me on the back and started to giggle.

I uttered a low growl and balled my hands into tight fists. But I didn't say anything. I could feel my face burning. I knew that I was blushing.

"You're too easy to scare, Duane," Stephanie teased again. "Admit it."

"Let's just get back to the tour," I grumbled.

"No way, Duane. This is fun. Let's try the next room. Come on."

When she saw that I wasn't following her, she said, "I won't scare you like that anymore. Promise."

I saw that her fingers were crossed. But I followed her anyway.

What choice did I have?

We crept through the narrow hall that connected us to the next room. And found ourselves in Andrew's room. Poor, headless Andrew.

It still had all his old stuff in it. Games and toys from a hundred years ago. An old-fashioned wooden bicycle leaning against one wall.

Everything just the way it was. Before Andrew met up with the sea captain's ghost.

A lantern on the dresser cast blue shadows on the walls. I didn't know if I believed the ghost story or not. But something told me that if Andrew's head were anywhere, we'd find it here. In his room.

Under his old-fashioned-looking canopy bed. Or hidden under his dusty, faded toys.

Stephanie tiptoed over to the toys. She bent down and started to move things aside. Little wooden bowling pins. An old-fashioned board game, the colors all faded to brown. A set of metal toy soldiers.

"Check around the bed, Duane," she whispered.

I started across the room. "Steph, we shouldn't be touching this stuff. You know the tour guides never let us touch anything."

Stephanie set down an old wooden top. "Do you want to find the head or not?"

"You really think there's a ghost's head hidden in this house?"

"Duane, that's what we're here to find out — right?"

I sighed and stepped over to the bed. I could see there was no use arguing with Stephanie tonight.

I ducked my head under the purple canopy and studied the bed. A boy actually slept in this bed, I told myself.

Andrew actually slept under this quilt. A hundred years ago.

The thought gave me a chill.

I tried to picture a boy about my age sleeping in this heavy, old bed.

"Go ahead. Check out the bed," Stephanie instructed from across the room.

I leaned over and patted the gray and brown patchwork quilt. It felt cold and smooth.

I punched the pillows. They felt soft and feathery. Nothing hidden inside the pillow cases.

I was about to test the mattress when the quilt began to move.

It rustled over the sheets. A soft, scratchy sound.

Then, as I stared in horror, the gray and brown quilt began to slide down the bed.

There was no one in the bed. No one!

But someone was pushing the quilt down, down to the bottom of the bed.

11

I swallowed a scream.

"You've got to move faster, Duane," Stephanie said.

I turned and saw her standing at the end of the bed. Holding the bottom of the quilt in both hands.

"We don't have all night!" she declared. She pulled the quilt down farther. "Nothing in the bed. Come on. Let's move on."

A sigh escaped my lips. Stephanie had tugged down the quilt and scared me again.

No ghost in the bed. No ghost pushing down the covers to climb out and grab me.

Only Stephanie.

At least this time she hadn't seen how frightened I was.

We worked together to pull the quilt back into place. She smiled at me. "This is kind of fun," she said.

"For sure," I agreed. I hoped she couldn't see that I was still shaking. "It's a lot more fun than tossing rubber spiders into Ben Fuller's bedroom window."

"I like being in this house so late at night. I like sneaking off from the group. I can feel a ghost lurking nearby," Stephanie whispered.

"You c-can?" I stammered, glancing quickly around the room.

My eyes stopped at the bottom of the door to the hallway.

There it sat. On the floor. Wedged between the door and the wall. Half-hidden in deep shadow.

The head.

This time, I saw the head.

Not a joke. Not a cruel trick.

Through the gray-black shadows, I saw the round skull. And I saw the two black eye sockets. Empty eye sockets. Two dark holes in the skull.

Staring up at me.

Staring.

I grabbed Stephanie's arm. I started to point. But there was no need.

Stephanie saw it, too.

12

I was the first to move. I took a step toward the door. Then another.

I heard sharp gasps. Someone breathing hard. Close behind me.

It took me a few seconds to realize it was Stephanie.

Keeping my eyes on the head, I made my way into the dark corner. My heart started to pound as I bent down and reached for it with both hands.

The black eye sockets stared up at me. Round, sad eyes.

My hands trembled.

I started to scoop it up.

But it slipped out of my hands. And started to roll away.

Stephanie let out a cry as the head rolled over the floor toward her.

In the orange light from the lantern, I saw her frightened expression. I saw that she was frozen there.

The head rolled over the floor and bumped against her sneaker. It came to a stop inches in front of her.

The empty black eye sockets stared up at her.

"Duane — " she called, staring down at it, hands pressed against her cheeks. "I didn't think — I didn't really think we'd find it. I — I — "

I hurried back across the room. It's my turn to be the brave one, I decided. My turn to show Stephanie that I'm not a wimp who's afraid of every shadow.

My turn to show Stephanie.

I scooped up the ghost's head in both hands. I raised it in front of Stephanie. Then I moved toward the lantern on the dressertop.

The head felt hard. Smoother than I thought.

The eye sockets were deep.

Stephanie stayed close by my side. Together we made our way into the orange lantern light.

I let out a groan when I realized I wasn't carrying a ghost's head.

Stephanie groaned too when she saw what I held in my hands.

13

A bowling ball.

I was carrying an old wooden bowling ball, the pale wood cracked and chipped.

"I don't believe it," Stephanie murmured, slapping her forehead.

My eyes went to the wooden bowling pins, lying among Andrew's old toys. "This must be the ball that went with those pins," I said softly.

Stephanie grabbed it from me and turned it between her hands. "But it only has two holes."

I nodded. "Yeah. In those days, bowling balls only had two holes. My dad told me about it one day when we went bowling. Dad never could figure out what they did with their thumb."

Stephanie stuck her fingers into the two holes. The "eye sockets." She shook her head. I could see she was really disappointed.

We could hear Otto's voice, booming from somewhere downstairs.

Stephanie sighed. "Maybe we should go down

and rejoin the tour," she suggested. She rolled the ball back to the pile of toys.

"No way!" I exclaimed.

I liked being the brave one for a change. I didn't want to quit while I was ahead.

"It's getting kind of late," Stephanie said. "And we're not going to find any ghost head up here."

"That's because we've already explored these rooms a hundred times," I told her. "I think we should find a room we've never explored before."

She scrunched up her face, thinking hard. "Duane, do you mean — ?"

"I mean, the ghost head is probably hidden in a room the tour doesn't go through. Maybe upstairs. You know. On the top floor."

Stephanie's eyes grew wide. "You want to sneak up to the top floor?"

I nodded. "Why not? That's probably where all the ghosts hang out — right?"

She studied me, her eyes searching mine. I knew she was surprised by my brave idea.

Of course, I didn't feel very brave at all. I just wanted to impress her. I just wanted to be the brave one for a change.

I was hoping that she'd say no. I was hoping she'd say, "Let's go back downstairs, Duane."

But instead, an excited grin spread over her face. And she said, "Okay. Let's do it!"

14

So I was stuck being the brave one.

We both had to be brave now. The Twin Terrors, on their way up the dark, creaking stairway that led to the third floor.

A sign beside the stairs read: NO VISITORS.

We stepped right past it and began climbing the narrow staircase. Side by side.

I couldn't hear Otto's voice anymore. Now I could only hear the creak and squeak of the steps beneath our sneakers. And the steady *thud thud thud* of my heart.

The air grew hot and damp as we reached the top. I squinted down a long, dark hallway. There were no lanterns. No candles.

The only light came from the window at the end of the hall. Pale light from outside that cast everything in an eerie, ghostly blue.

"Let's start in the first room," Stephanie suggested, whispering. She brushed her dark hair off her face.

It was so hot up here, I had sweat running down my forehead. I mopped it up with my jacket sleeve and followed Stephanie to the first room on the right.

The heavy wooden door was half open. We slid in through the opening. Pale blue light washed in through the dust-caked windows.

I waited for my eyes to adjust. Then I squinted around the large room.

Empty. Completely empty. No furniture. No sign of life.

Or ghosts.

"Steph — look." I pointed to a narrow door against the far wall. "Let's check it out."

We crept across the bare floor. Through the dusty window, I glimpsed the full moon, high over the bare trees now.

The doorway led to another room. Smaller and even warmer. A steam radiator clanked against one wall. Two old-fashioned-looking couches stood facing each other in the center of the room. No other furniture.

"Let's keep moving," Stephanie whispered.

Another narrow door led to another dark room. "The rooms up here are all connected," I murmured. I sneezed. Sneezed again.

"Ssshhh. Quiet, Duane," Stephanie scolded. "The ghosts will hear us coming."

"I can't help it," I protested. "It's so dusty up here."

We were in some kind of sewing room. An old sewing machine stood on a table in front of the window. A carton at my feet was filled with balls of black yarn.

I bent down and pawed quickly through the balls of yarn. No head hidden in there.

We stepped into the next room before we realized it was completely dark.

The window was partly shuttered. Only a tiny square of gray light crept through from outside.

"I-I can't see anything," Stephanie declared. I felt her hand grasp my arm. "It's too dark. Let's get out of here, Duane."

I started to reply. But a loud *thump* made my breath catch in my throat.

Stephanie's hand squeezed my hand. "Duane, did you make that *thump*?"

Another *thump*. Closer to us.

"No. Not m-me," I stammered.

Another *thump* on the floor.

"We're not alone in here," Stephanie whispered.

I took a deep breath. "Who is it?" I called. "Who's there?"

15

"Who's there?" I choked out.

Stephanie squeezed my arm so hard, it hurt. But I made no attempt to move away from her.

I heard soft footsteps. Ghostly footsteps.

A cold chill froze the back of my neck. I clamped my jaw shut to keep my teeth from chattering.

And then yellow eyes floated toward us through the thick darkness.

Four yellow eyes.

The creature had *four* eyes!

A gurgling sound escaped my throat. I couldn't breathe. I couldn't move.

I stared straight ahead. Listening.

Watching.

The eyes floated apart in pairs. Two eyes moved to the right, two to the left.

"Noooo!" I cried out when I saw more eyes.

Yellow eyes in the corners of the room. Evil eyes glinting at us from against the wall.

Yellow eyes all along the floor.

Yellow eyes all around us.

Catlike yellow eyes glaring in silence at Stephanie and me as we huddled together in the center of the room.

Catlike eyes.

Cat's eyes.

Because the room was filled with cats.

A shrill *yowl* gave them away. A long *meeee-yoww* from the windowsill made Stephanie and me both sigh in relief.

A cat brushed against my leg. Startled, I jumped aside, bumping into Stephanie.

She bumped me back.

More cats meowed. Another cat brushed the back of my jeans leg.

"I-I think these cats are lonely," Stephanie stammered. "Do you think anyone ever comes up here?"

"I don't care," I snapped. "All these yellow eyes floating around. I thought . . . I thought . . . well . . . I don't know *what* I thought! It's creepy. Let's get out of here."

For once, Stephanie didn't argue.

She led the way to the door at the back of the room. All around us, cats were howling and yowling.

Another one brushed my leg.

Stephanie tripped over a cat. In the darkness, I saw her fall. She landed on her knees with a hard *thud*.

The cats all began to screech.

"Are you okay?" I cried, hurrying to help pull her up.

The cats were howling so loud, I couldn't hear her reply.

We jogged to the door, pulled it open, and escaped.

I closed the door behind us. Silence now. "Where are we?" I whispered.

"I-I don't know," Stephanie stammered, keeping close to the wall.

I moved to a tall, narrow window and peered through the dusty glass. The window led out to a small balcony. The balcony jutted out from the gray shingled roof.

Pale white moonlight washed in through the window.

I turned back to Stephanie. "We're in some kind of back hallway," I guessed. The long, narrow hallway seemed to stretch on forever. "Maybe these rooms are used by the workers. You know. Manny, the night watchman. The house cleaners. And the tour guides."

Stephanie sighed. She stared down the long hallway. "Let's go downstairs and find Otto and the tour group. I think we've done enough exploring for tonight."

I agreed. "There must be stairs at the end of this hall. Let's go."

I took four or five steps. Then I felt the ghostly hands.

They brushed over my face. My neck. My body. Sticky, dry, invisible hands.

The hands pushed me back as they clung to my skin.

"Ohhhh, help!" Stephanie moaned.

The ghosts had her in their grasp, too.

16

The ghost's filmy hands brushed over me. I could feel the soft fingers — dry and soft as air — tighten around my skin.

Stephanie's hands thrashed wildly. Beside me in the dark hall, she struggled to free herself.

"It-it's like a net!" she choked out.

I swiped at my face. My hair.

I spun away. But the dry fingers clung to me. Tightening. Tightening.

And I realized we hadn't walked into a ghost's grasp.

Tugging and tearing frantically with both hands, I realized we had walked into cobwebs.

A thick curtain of cobwebs.

The blanket of sticky threads had fallen over us like a fisherman's net. The more we struggled, the tighter it wrapped itself around us.

"Stephanie — it's *cobwebs*!" I cried. I tugged a thick, stringy wad of them off my face.

"Of course it's cobwebs!" she shot back, squirming and thrashing. "What did *you* think it was?"

"Uh . . . a ghost," I muttered.

Stephanie snickered. "Duane, I know you have a good imagination. But if you start seeing ghosts *everywhere*, we'll never get out of here."

"I . . . I . . . I . . ." I didn't know what to say.

Stephanie thought the same thing I did. She thought she'd been grabbed by a ghost. But now she was pretending she knew all along.

We stood there in the darkness, tearing the sticky threads off our faces and arms and bodies. I let out an angry groan. I couldn't brush the stuff from my hair!

"I'm going to itch *forever*!" I wailed.

"I've got more bad news for you," Stephanie murmured.

I pulled a thick wad off my ear. "Huh?"

"Who do you think made these cobwebs?"

I didn't have to think about it. "Spiders?"

My arms and legs started to tingle. My back began to itch. I felt a light tingling on the back of my neck.

Were there spiders crawling up and down my body? Hundreds and hundreds of them?

Forgetting the wispy strings of cobweb, I started to run. Stephanie had the same idea. We both ran down the long hall, scratching and slapping at ourselves.

"Steph — the next time you have a great idea, *don't* have a great idea!" I warned her.

"Let's just get out of here!" she groaned.

We reached the end of the hall, still scratching as we ran.

No stairway.

How do we get back downstairs?

Another hall twisted to the left. Low candles over the doorways flickered and danced. Shadows darted over the worn carpet like slithering animals.

"Come on." I pulled Stephanie's arm. We had no choice. We had to follow this hallway, too.

We jogged side by side. The rooms were all dark and silent.

The candle flames dipped as we ran past. Our long shadows ran ahead of us, as if eager to get downstairs first.

I stopped when I heard someone laughing.

"Whoa," Stephanie murmured, breathing hard. Her dark eyes grew wide.

We both listened hard.

I heard voices. Inside the room at the end of the hall.

The door was closed. I couldn't make out the words. I heard a man say something. A woman laughed. Other people laughed.

"We caught up to the tour," I whispered.

Stephanie scrunched up her face. "But the tour never comes up here to the top floor," she protested.

We stepped up close to the door and listened again.

More laughter on the other side. A lot of people talking cheerfully, all at the same time. It sounded like a party.

I pressed my ear against the door. "I think the tour ended, and everyone is just chatting," I whispered.

Stephanie scratched the back of her neck. She pulled a stringy gob of cobweb from her hair. "Well, hurry, Duane. Open the door. Let's join them," she urged.

"I hope Otto doesn't ask us where we've been," I replied.

I grabbed the doorknob and pushed open the door.

Stephanie and I took a step inside.

And gasped in shock at what we saw.

17

The room stood empty.

Empty, silent, and dark.

"What happened? Where is everyone?" Stephanie cried.

We took another step into the dark room. The floor creaked beneath us. The only sound.

"I don't get it," Stephanie whispered. "Didn't we just hear voices in here?"

"Lots," I said. "They were laughing and talking. It really sounded like a party."

"A big party," Stephanie added, her eyes darting around the empty room. "Tons of people."

A cold chill ran down the back of my neck. "I don't think we heard people," I whispered.

Stephanie turned to me. "Huh?"

"They weren't people," I croaked. "They were ghosts."

Her mouth dropped open. "And they all disappeared when we opened the door?"

I nodded. "I — I think I can still feel them in here. I can feel their presence."

Stephanie let out a frightened squeak. "Feel them? What do you mean?"

At that moment, a cold wind came whooshing through the room. It rushed over me, cold and dry. And it chilled me down to my toes.

Stephanie must have felt it, too. She wrapped her arms around her chest. "Brrr! Do you feel that breeze? Is the window open? How come it got so cold in here all of a sudden?" she asked.

She shivered again. Her voice became tiny. "We're not alone in here, are we?"

"I don't think so," I whispered. "I think we just crashed someone's party."

Stephanie and I stood there, feeling the cold of the room. I didn't dare move. Maybe a ghost stood right beside me. Maybe the ghosts we heard were all around us, staring at us, preparing to swoop over us.

"Stephanie," I whispered. "What if we really have crashed their party? What if we've invaded the ghosts' quarters?"

Stephanie swallowed hard. She didn't reply.

Hadn't Andrew, the ghost boy, lost his head when he stumbled into the ghost's living quarters? Were we standing in the same living quarters? The same room where Andrew found the ghost of the old sea captain?

"Stephanie, I think we should get out of here," I said softly. "Now."

I wanted to run. I wanted to fly down the stairs. Fly out of Hill House. Fly to my safe, warm home where there were no ghosts.

No ghosts.

We spun around and bolted for the door.

Were the ghosts going to try to stop us?

No. We made it back into the flickering orange light of the hallway. I pulled the door shut behind us.

"The stairs. Where are the stairs?" Stephanie cried.

We stood at the end of the hall. Facing a solid wall. The flowers on the wallpaper appeared to open and close, moving in the darting candlelight.

I banged both fists against the wall. "How do we get out of here? How?"

Stephanie had already pulled open a door across the hall. I followed her inside.

"Oh, no!" Ghostly figures filled the room. It took me a few seconds to realize that I was staring at sheets pulled over furniture. Chairs and couches covered with sheets.

"M-maybe this is the ghosts' living room," I stammered.

Stephanie didn't hear me. She had already burst through the open door against the far wall.

I followed her into another room, cluttered with

large crates. The crates were piled nearly to the ceiling.

Another room. Then another.

My heart began to pound. My throat ached.

I felt so discouraged. Were we ever going to find our way to the stairs?

Another door. Another dark, empty room.

"Hey, Steph — " I whispered. "I think we're going in circles."

Out into a long, twisting hallway. More candles. More flowers flickering darkly on the wallpaper.

We ran side by side down the hall. Until we came to a door I hadn't seen before. A door with a horseshoe nailed onto it.

Maybe it meant that our luck was about to change. I sure hoped so!

I grabbed the knob with a trembling hand. I pulled open the door.

A staircase!

"Yes!" I cried.

"Finally!" Stephanie gasped.

"This must be the servants' staircase," I guessed. "Maybe we've been in the servants' quarters all this time."

The stairway was blanketed in darkness. The stairs looked steep.

I took a step down, holding onto the wall. Then another step.

Stephanie had one hand on my shoulder. When I stepped down, she stepped down, too.

Another step. Another. The soft *thud*s of our sneakers echoed in the deep stairwell.

We had taken about ten steps when I heard footsteps.

Someone coming up the stairs.

18

Stephanie bumped me hard. I shot out both hands. Grabbed the wall to keep from falling down the stairs.

No time to turn and run.

The footsteps grew louder. And heavier. Light from a flashlight swept over Stephanie, then me.

Squinting against the light, I saw a dark figure climbing up to us. "So *there* you are!" his voice boomed, echoing in the stairwell.

A familiar voice.

"Otto!" Stephanie and I both cried.

He bounced up in front of us, moving the flashlight from her face to mine. "What are you two doing up here?" he demanded breathlessly.

"Uh . . . we got lost," I answered quickly.

"We got separated from the tour," Stephanie added. "We tried to find you."

"Yes. We tried," I chimed in. "We were searching everywhere. But we couldn't catch up to the group."

Otto lowered the flashlight. I could see his tiny dark eyes narrowing at us. I don't think he believed our story.

"I thought you two knew my tour by heart," he said, rubbing his chin.

"We do," Stephanie insisted. "We just got turned around. We got lost. And we — "

"But how did you get up here on the top floor?" Otto demanded.

"Well . . ." I started. But I couldn't think of a good answer. I turned back to Stephanie on the step above me.

"We heard voices up here. We thought it was you," she told Otto.

It wasn't exactly a lie. We *did* hear voices.

Otto lowered the beam of light to the stairs. "Well, let's get back downstairs. No one is allowed on this floor. It's private."

"Sorry," Stephanie and I murmured.

"Watch your step, kids," Otto warned. "These back stairs are very steep and rickety. I'll lead you back to the group. Edna took over for me while I went to find you."

Edna was our second-favorite tour guide. She was old and white-haired. Very pale and frail-looking, especially in her black tour-guide outfit.

But she was a great storyteller. With her quivering, old voice, she really made you *believe* every frightening story she told.

Stephanie and I eagerly clumped down the stairs, following Otto. His flashlight swept in front of us as he led us out onto the second floor. We followed a long hallway. A hallway I knew very well.

We stopped outside Joseph Craw's study. Joseph was Andrew's father. I peeked inside. A bright fire blazed in the fireplace.

Edna stood beside the fireplace, telling the tragic story of Joseph Craw to the tour group.

Stephanie and I had heard the sad story a hundred times. A year after Andrew had his head cut off, Joseph came home late one winter night. He took off his coat, then moved to the fireplace to warm himself.

No one knows how Joseph was burned up. At least, that's how Otto, Edna, and the other guides tell the story. Was he pushed into the fireplace? Did he fall in?

One guess is as good as another.

But when the maid came into the study the next morning, she found a horrifying sight.

She found two charred, blackened hands gripping the mantel.

Two hands, holding on tightly to the marble mantelpiece.

All that was left of Joseph Craw.

It's a yucky story — isn't it?

It gives me a chill every time I hear it.

As Otto led us to the study, Edna was just getting to the sickening part. The ending. "Do you want to rejoin the group?" Otto whispered.

"It's pretty late. I think we'd better get home," Stephanie told him.

I quickly agreed. "Thanks for rescuing us. We'll catch the tour again soon."

"Good night," Otto said, clicking off his flashlight. "You know the way out." He hurried into the study.

I started to leave. But stopped when I saw the boy again, the pale boy with the wavy blond hair. The boy in the black jeans and black turtleneck.

He stood away from the tour group. Close to the door. And he was staring at Stephanie and me again. Staring hard at us, a cold expression on his face.

"Come on," I whispered, grabbing Stephanie's arm. I tugged her away from the study door.

We quickly found the front stairway. A few seconds later, we pushed open the front door and stepped outside. A cold wind greeted us as we started down the hill. Wisps of black cloud floated like snakes over the moon.

"Well, that was fun!" Stephanie declared. She zipped her coat to her chin.

"Fun?" I wasn't so sure. "It was kind of scary."

Stephanie grinned at me. "But we weren't afraid — right?"

I shivered. "Right."

"I'd like to go back and explore some more," she said. "You know. Maybe go back to that room with all the voices. Find some real ghosts."

"Yeah. Great," I agreed. I didn't feel like arguing with her. I felt pretty tired.

She pulled a wool muffler from her coat pocket. As she swung it around her neck, one end caught in a low pine bush.

"Hey — !" she cried out.

I moved to the bush and started to pull the muffler free.

And that's when I heard the voice.

Just a whisper. A whisper from the other side of the bush.

But I heard it very clearly.

"Did you find my head?"

That's what I heard.

"Did you find my head? Did you find it for me?"

19

I uttered a startled gasp and stared into the bush. "Stephanie — did you hear that?" I choked out.

No reply.

"Stephanie? Steph?"

I spun around. She was staring at me, her mouth open in surprise.

"Did you hear that whisper?" I asked again.

Then I realized she wasn't staring at me. She was staring past me.

I turned — and saw the strange, blond boy standing there beside the pine bush. "Hey — did you just whisper to us?" I demanded sharply.

He narrowed his pale gray eyes at me. "Huh? Me?"

"Yeah. You," I snapped. "Were you trying to scare us?"

He shook his head. "No way."

"You didn't whisper from behind this bush?" I asked again.

"I just got out here," the boy insisted.

We saw him in Joseph Craw's study less than a minute ago, I told myself. How did he get out here so fast?

"Why did you follow us?" Stephanie demanded, shoving her muffler around her coat collar.

The boy shrugged.

"Why were you staring at us?" I asked, stepping up close to Stephanie.

The wind howled over the hilltop. The row of pine bushes shook in the gusty wind, as if shivering. Thin black clouds continued to snake their way over the pale moon.

The boy wore no coat. Only the black turtleneck and black jeans. The wind fluttered his long, wavy hair.

"We saw you staring at us," Stephanie repeated. "How come?"

He shrugged again. He kept his strange, gray eyes down at the ground. "I saw you sneak away," he said. "I wondered if . . . if you saw anything interesting."

"We got lost," I told him, glancing at Stephanie. "We didn't see much."

"What's your name?" Stephanie asked.

"Seth," he replied.

We told him our names.

"Do you live in Wheeler Falls?" Stephanie asked.

He shook his head. He kept his eyes down at his shoes. "No. I'm just visiting."

Why wouldn't he look us in the eye? Was he just shy?

"Are you sure you didn't whisper something from behind that bush?" I asked again.

He shook his head. "No way. Maybe someone was playing a joke on you."

"Maybe," I said. I stepped closer and kicked the bush. I don't know what I expected.

But nothing happened.

"You and Stephanie went exploring on your own?" Seth asked.

"Yeah. A little," I confessed. "We're kind of into ghosts."

When I said that, he jerked his head up. He raised his gray eyes and gazed hard at Stephanie, then at me.

His face had been a blank. No life to it. No expression at all.

But now I could see that he was really excited.

"Do you want to see some real ghosts?" he asked us, staring hard. "Do you?"

20

Seth stared at us as if challenging us. "Do you two want to see some real ghosts?"

"Yeah. Sure," Stephanie replied, returning his stare.

"What do you mean, Seth?" I demanded. "Have *you* ever seen a ghost?"

He nodded. "Yeah. In there." He pointed with his head, back to the big stone house.

"Huh?" I cried. "You saw a real ghost in Hill House? When?"

"Duane and I have taken the tour a hundred times," Stephanie told him. "We've never seen any ghost in there."

He snickered. "Of course not. Do you think the ghosts come out when the tour groups are in there? They wait till the house closes. They wait until all the tourists go home."

"How do *you* know?" I asked.

"I sneaked in," Seth replied. "Late one night."

"You *what*?" I cried. "How?"

"I found a door around back. It was unlocked. I guess everyone forgot about it," Seth explained. "I sneaked in after the house was closed. And I — "

He stopped suddenly. His eyes were on the house.

I turned and saw the front door open. People stepped out, fastening their coats. The last tour had ended. People were heading for home.

"Over here!" Seth whispered.

We followed him behind the pine bushes and ducked down low. The people walked past us. They were laughing and talking about the house and all the ghost stories.

When they were down the hill, we stood up again. Seth brushed his long hair off his forehead. But the wind blew it right back.

"I sneaked in late at night, when the house was dark," he repeated.

"Your parents let you go out so late at night?" I asked.

A strange smile crossed his lips. "They didn't know," he said softly. The smile faded. "Your parents let you two out?"

Stephanie laughed. "Our parents don't know, either."

"Good," Seth replied.

"And you really saw a ghost?" I asked.

He nodded. Brushed his hair back again. "I crept past Manny, the night watchman. He was sound asleep. Snoring away. I made my way to the front of the house. I was standing at the bottom of the big staircase — when I heard a laugh."

I gulped. "A laugh?"

"From the top of the stairs. I backed up against the wall. And I saw the ghost. A very old lady. In a long dress and a black bonnet. She wore a heavy black veil over the front of her face. But I could see her eyes through the veil. I could see them because they glowed bright red — like fire!"

"Wow!" Stephanie cried. "What did she do?"

Seth turned to the house. The front door had closed. The lantern over the door had been put out. The house stood in total darkness.

"The old ghost came sliding down the banister," he reported. "She tossed back her head — and screamed all the way down. And as she slid, her red eyes left a bright trail, like the tail of a comet."

"Weren't you scared?" I asked Seth. "Didn't you try to run away?"

"There was no time," he replied. "She came sliding down the banister, right toward me. Eyes blazing. Screaming like some kind of crazed animal. I was pressed against the wall. I couldn't move. And when she reached the bottom, I thought she'd grab me. But she vanished. Disappeared into the darkness. And all that was left was the faint red glow, floating in the air. The glow of her eyes."

"Oh, wow!" Stephanie cried.

"That's *awesome!*" I agreed.

"I want to sneak back in again," Seth declared, watching the house. "I'll bet there are more ghosts in there. I really want to see them."

"Me, too!" Stephanie cried eagerly.

Seth smiled at her. "So you'll come with me? Tomorrow night? I don't want to go back alone. It'll be so much more fun if you come, too."

The wind swirled sharply. The black clouds rolled over the moon, covering it, shutting out its light. The old house appeared to grow darker on its hilltop perch.

"So you'll come with me tomorrow night?" Seth asked again.

"Yeah. Great!" Stephanie told him. "I can't wait. How about you, Duane?" She turned to me. "You'll come, too — won't you, Duane? Won't you?"

70

21

I said yes.

I said I couldn't wait to see a real ghost.

I said I was shivering because of the cold wind. Not because I was scared.

We made a plan to meet at midnight tomorrow at the back of Hill House. Then Seth hurried away. And Stephanie and I walked home.

The street was dark and empty. Most of the house lights were out. Far in the distance, a dog howled.

Stephanie and I walked quickly, leaning into the wind. We usually didn't stay out this late.

Tomorrow night, we'd be even later.

"I don't trust that guy," I told Stephanie as we reached her front yard. "He's too weird."

I expected her to agree. But she said, "You're just jealous, Duane."

"Huh? Me? Jealous?" I couldn't believe she said that. "Why would I be jealous?"

"Because Seth is so brave. Because he saw a ghost and we didn't."

I shook my head. "Do you believe that crazy story about a ghost sliding down the banister? I think he made it up."

"Well," Stephanie replied thoughtfully, "we'll find out tomorrow night — won't we!"

Tomorrow night came too quickly.

I had a math test in the afternoon. I don't think I did too well on it. I couldn't stop thinking about Seth, and Hill House, and ghosts.

After dinner, Mom cornered me in the living room. She brushed back my hair and studied my face. "Why do you look so tired?" she asked. "You have dark circles around your eyes."

"Maybe I'm part raccoon," I replied. That's what I always say when she tells me I have circles around my eyes.

"I think you should go to bed early tonight," Dad chimed in. Dad always thinks that everyone should go to bed early.

So I went to my room at nine-thirty. But of course I didn't go to sleep.

I read a book and listened to a tape on my Walkman. And waited for Mom and Dad to go to bed. And watched the clock.

Mom and Dad are very heavy sleepers. You can pound and pound on their bedroom door, and they don't wake up. They once slept through a hurricane. That's the truth. They didn't hear the tree that fell onto our house!

Stephanie's parents are heavy sleepers, too. That's why it's so easy for the two of us to sneak out of our bedroom windows. That's why it's so easy for us to haunt our neighborhood at night.

As the clock neared midnight, I wished we were going out on one of our usual haunting trips. I wished we were going to hide under Chrissy Jacob's window and howl like wolves. And then toss rubber spiders into Ben Fuller's bed.

But Stephanie had decided that was too boring.

We needed excitement. We needed to go ghost hunting. With a strange kid we'd never seen before.

At ten to twelve, I pulled on my down coat and crept out of my bedroom window. Another cold, windy night. I felt sprinkles of frozen rain on my forehead. So I pulled up my hood.

Stephanie was waiting for me at the bottom of her driveway. She had pulled her brown hair back in a ponytail. Her coat was open. She wore a heavy ski sweater underneath, pulled down over her jeans.

She raised her head and let out a ghostly howl. *"Owooooooo!"*

I clapped my hand over her open mouth. "You'll wake up the whole block!"

She laughed and backed away from me. "I'm a little excited. Aren't you?" She opened her mouth in another howl.

The frozen rain pattered the ground. We hurried toward Hill House. The swirling wind scattered twigs and dead leaves as we walked. Most of the house lights had been turned off.

A car rolled by slowly as we turned onto Hill Street. Stephanie and I ducked behind a hedge. The driver might wonder why two kids were wandering around Wheeler Falls at midnight.

I wondered, too.

We waited for the car to disappear. Then we continued our journey.

Our sneakers crunched over the hard ground as we climbed the hill that led to the old haunted house. Hill House rose above us, like a silent monster waiting to swallow us up.

The last tour had ended. The lights were all off. Otto and Edna and the other tour guides were probably all home by now.

"Come on, Duane. Hurry," Stephanie urged. She started to run around the side of the house. "Seth is probably waiting."

"Wait up!" I cried. We followed a narrow dirt path around to the back.

Squinting into the darkness, I searched for Seth. No sign of him.

The backyard was cluttered with equipment of all kinds. A row of rusted metal trashcans formed a fence along one wall. A long wooden ladder lay on its side in the tall weeds. Wooden cartons and barrels and cardboard boxes were strewn everywhere. A hand lawnmower tilted against the house.

"It — it's so much darker back here," Stephanie stammered. "Do you see Seth?"

"I can't see *anything*," I replied in a whisper. "Maybe he changed his mind. Maybe he isn't coming."

Stephanie started to reply. But a choked cry from the side of the house made us both jump.

I turned to see Seth stagger into view.

His blond hair was wild, flying around his face. His eyes bulged. His hands gripped his throat.

"The ghost!" he cried, stumbling clumsily. "The ghost — he — he *got* me!"

Then Seth collapsed at our feet and didn't move.

22

"Nice try, Seth," I said calmly.

"Nice fall," Stephanie added.

He raised his head slowly, staring up at us. "I didn't fool you?"

"No way," I replied.

Stephanie rolled her eyes. "That's Joke Number One," she told Seth. "Duane and I have pulled that one a thousand times."

Seth climbed to his feet and brushed off the front of his black turtleneck. He scowled, disappointed. "Just trying to give you a little scare."

"You'll have to do better than that," I told him.

"Duane and I are experts at giving scares," Stephanie added. "It's sort of our hobby."

Seth straightened his hair with both hands. "You two are weird," he murmured.

I brushed cold raindrops off my eyebrows. "Can we get inside?" I asked impatiently.

Seth led the way to the narrow door at the far

side of the house. "Did you two have any trouble sneaking out?" he asked, whispering.

"No. No trouble," Stephanie told him.

"Neither did I," he replied. He stepped up to the door and lifted the wooden latch. "I took the tour again tonight," he whispered. "Otto showed me some new things. Some new rooms we can explore."

"Great!" Stephanie exclaimed. "Do you promise we'll see a real ghost?"

Seth turned back to her. A strange smile spread over his face. "Promise," he said.

23

Seth gave the door a tug, and it creaked open.

We slipped inside. Into total blackness. Too dark to see where we were.

I took a few steps into the room — and bumped into Seth.

"Ssshhh," he warned. "Manny the night watchman is posted in the front room. He's probably asleep already. But we'd better stay in back."

"Where are we?" I whispered.

"In one of the back rooms," Seth whispered. "Wait a few seconds. Our eyes will adjust."

"Can't we turn on a light?" I asked.

"Ghosts won't come out in the light," Seth replied.

We had closed the door behind us. But a cold wind still blew at my back.

I shivered.

A soft rattling sound made my breath catch in my throat.

Was I starting to hear things?

I pulled off my hood to hear better.

Silence now.

"I think I know where I can find some candles," Seth whispered. "You two wait here. Don't move."

"D-don't worry," I stammered. I didn't plan to go anywhere until I could see!

I heard Seth move away, making soft, scraping footsteps over the floor, keeping as quiet as he could. His footsteps faded into silence.

Then I felt another rush of cold wind against the back of my neck.

"Oh!" I cried out when I heard the rattling again.

A gentle rattling. Like the rattling of bones.

Another cold gust of wind swept over me. A ghost's cold breath, I thought. My whole body shook as a chill ran down my back.

I heard the rattling bones again. Louder. A clattering sound. So close.

I reached out in the thick blackness. Tried to grab onto a wall. Or a table. Or anything.

But my hands grabbed only air.

I swallowed hard. Calm down, Duane, I ordered myself. Seth will be back in a moment with some candles. Then you'll see that everything is okay.

But another jangle and clatter of bones made me gasp.

"Steph — did you hear that?" I whispered.

No reply.

A cold wind tingled my neck.

The bones rattled again.

"Steph? Do you hear that noise, too? Steph?"

No reply.

"Stephanie? Steph?" I called.

She was gone.

24

Panic time.

My breaths came short and fast. My heart clattered louder than the skeleton bones. My whole body began to shake.

"Stephanie? Steph? Where *are* you?" I choked out weakly.

Then I saw the two yellow eyes moving toward me. Two glowing eyes, floating silently, gleaming with evil. Coming nearer. Nearer.

I froze.

I couldn't move. I couldn't see anything but those two gleaming, yellow eyes.

"Ohh!" I uttered a moan as they floated closer. And I could see them more clearly. See that they were candle flames.

Two candle flames, moving side by side.

In the soft yellow light, I saw Seth's face. And Stephanie's. They each carried a lighted candle in front of them.

"Stephanie — where *were* you?" I cried in a choked whisper. "I — I thought — "

"I went with Seth," she replied calmly.

The orange glow from her candle washed over me. I guess Stephanie could see how panicked I was. "I'm sorry, Duane," she said softly. "I said I was going with Seth. I thought you heard me."

"S-something is rattling," I stammered. "Bones, I think. I keep feeling a cold wind, and I keep hearing — "

Seth handed me a candle. "Light it," he instructed. "We'll look around. See what's rattling."

I took the candle and raised it to his. But my hand was shaking so badly, it took me five tries to light the wick. Finally, the candle flamed to life.

I gazed around in the flickering orange light.

"Hey — we're in the kitchen," Stephanie whispered.

A gust of cold wind blew past me. "Did you feel that?" I cried.

Seth pointed his candle flame toward the kitchen window. "Look, Duane — that window-pane. It's missing. The cold air is blowing in through the hole."

"Oh. Right."

Another blast of air. And then the rattling.

"Did you hear it?" I demanded.

Stephanie giggled. She pointed to the kitchen

wall. In the dim light, I saw big pots and pans hanging on the wall. "The wind is making them rattle," Stephanie explained.

"Ha-ha." I uttered a feeble laugh. "I knew that. I was just trying to scare you," I lied. "You know. Give you a thrill."

I felt like a total jerk. But why should I admit that a bunch of pots on the wall nearly had me scared out of my skin?

"Okay. No more jokes," Stephanie insisted, turning to Seth. "We want to see a real ghost."

"Follow me. I'll show you something that Otto told me about," Seth whispered.

Holding his candle in front of him, he led the way across the kitchen to the wall beside the stove. He lowered his candle in front of a cabinet door. Then he pulled open the cabinet door and moved the candle closer so we could see inside.

"Why are you showing us a kitchen cabinet?" I demanded. "What's scary about that?"

"It's not a cabinet," Seth replied. "It's a dumbwaiter. Watch." He reached inside and pulled a rope beside the cabinet shelf. The shelf began to slide up.

He raised the shelf, then lowered it. "See? This dumbwaiter is like a little elevator. It was used to send food from the kitchen to the master bedroom upstairs."

"You mean for midnight snacks?" I joked.

Seth nodded. "The cook would put the food on the shelf. Then he would pull the rope, and the shelf would carry it upstairs."

"Thrills and chills," I said sarcastically.

"Yeah. Why are you showing it to us?" Stephanie demanded.

Seth brought the candle up close to his face. "Otto told me that this dumbwaiter is haunted. A hundred and twenty years ago, things suddenly started to go wrong with it."

Stephanie and I moved closer. I lowered my candle and examined the dumbwaiter cabinet. "What went wrong?" I asked.

"Well," Seth began softly, "the cook would put food on the shelf and send it upstairs. But when the shelf reached the bedroom up there, the food was gone."

Stephanie narrowed her eyes at Seth. "It disappeared between the first and second floor?"

Seth nodded solemnly. His gray eyes glowed in the soft candlelight. "This happened several times. When the shelf reached the second floor, it was empty. The food had vanished."

"Wow," I murmured.

"The cook became very frightened," Seth continued. "He was afraid that the dumbwaiter had become haunted. He decided to stop using it. And he ordered everyone on his staff never to use the dumbwaiter again."

"And that's the end of the story?" I asked.

Seth shook his head. "And then something horrible happened."

Stephanie's mouth dropped open. "What? What happened?"

"Some kids were visiting the house. One of them was a boy named Jeremy. Jeremy was a real show-off, and very athletic. When he saw the dumbwaiter, he decided it would be fun to ride it to the second floor."

"Oh, wow," Stephanie murmured.

I felt a chill. I thought I could guess what was coming.

"So Jeremy squeezed onto the shelf. And one of the other kids pulled the rope. Suddenly the rope caught. The kid couldn't get it to move up or down. Jeremy was stuck somewhere between the floors.

"The other kids called up to him, 'Are you okay?' But Jeremy didn't reply. They started to get very worried. They tugged and tugged, but they couldn't move the rope.

"Then suddenly, the shelf came crashing back down."

"And was Jeremy on it?" I asked eagerly.

Seth shook his head. "There were three covered bowls on the shelf. The kids lifted the lid off the first bowl. Inside was Jeremy's heart, still beating.

"They opened the second bowl. Inside were Jeremy's eyes, still staring in horror. And they opened the third bowl. And saw Jeremy's teeth, still chattering."

The three of us stood silent in the orange glow of candlelight. We stared at the dumbwaiter shelf.

I shivered. The pots rattled against the wall. But I was no longer frightened by them. I raised my eyes to Seth. "Do you think that story is true?"

Stephanie laughed. Nervous laughter. "It can't be true," she said.

Seth's face remained solemn. "Do you believe *any* of Otto's stories?" he asked me quietly.

"Well. Yes. No. Some." I couldn't decide.

"Otto swears the story is true," Seth insisted. "But of course, he may just be doing his job. His job is to make this house as scary as possible."

"Otto is a great storyteller," Stephanie murmured. "But enough stories. I want to see a real ghost."

"Follow me," Seth replied. His candle flame dipped low as he spun around.

He led us back through the kitchen, into a long, narrow room at the back. "This is the old butler's pantry," he announced. "All of the food for the house was stored in here."

Stephanie and I stepped past him, raising our candles to see the room better. When I turned around, Seth was closing the pantry door behind us.

Then I saw him turn the lock.

"Hey — what are you doing?" I cried.

"Why are you locking us in here?" Stephanie demanded.

25

I dropped my candle. It bounced on the hard floor, and the flame went out. The candle rolled under a shelf.

When I glanced back up, Stephanie was storming toward Seth. "Seth — what are you doing?" she demanded angrily. "Unlock that door. This isn't funny!"

I gazed around the long, narrow room. Shelves from floor to ceiling on three walls. No windows. No other door to escape through.

With a sharp cry, Stephanie grabbed for the door handle. But Seth moved quickly to block her way.

"Hey — !" I cried, my heart pounding. I stepped up beside Stephanie. "What's the big idea, Seth?"

His silvery eyes glowed with excitement behind his candle flame. He stared back at us without speaking. The same cold stare I had seen on his face the night before.

Stephanie and I took a step back, huddling close together.

"Sorry, guys. But I played a little trick on you," he said finally.

"Excuse me?" Stephanie cried, more angry than frightened.

"What kind of trick?" I asked.

He pushed back his long, blond hair with his free hand. The flickering candle sent shadows dancing across his face. "My name isn't Seth," he said softly, so softly I could barely hear him.

"But — but — " I stammered.

"My name is Andrew," he said.

Stephanie and I both cried out in surprise.

"But Andrew is the name of the ghost," Stephanie protested. "The ghost who lost his head."

"I am the ghost," he said softly. A dry laugh escaped his lips. More like a cough than a laugh. "I promised you a real ghost tonight. Well . . . here I am."

He blew out the candle. He appeared to vanish with the light.

"But, Seth — " Stephanie started.

"Andrew," he corrected her. "My name is Andrew. My name has been Andrew for more than a hundred years."

"Let us out of here," I pleaded. "We won't tell anyone we saw you. We won't — "

"I can't let you go," he replied in a whisper.

I remembered the story of the sea captain's ghost. When Andrew stumbled into the sea captain's room and saw the old ghost, the sea captain had said the same thing to him. *"Now that you have seen me, I can never let you go."*

"You — you lost your head!" I blurted out.

"So you *can't* be Andrew!" Stephanie cried. "You have a head!"

In the dim light from Stephanie's candle, I could see the sneer spread over Andrew's face. "No," he said softly. "No, no, no. I do not have my head. This is one that I borrowed."

He raised both hands to the sides of his face. "Here. Let me show you," he said.

Then he pressed his hands against his cheeks and started to tug the head up from the black turtleneck.

26

"No! Stop!" Stephanie screeched.

I shut my eyes. I didn't really want to see him pull off his head.

When I opened my eyes, Andrew had lowered his hands.

I gazed once again around the narrow pantry. How could we escape? How could we get out of there? The ghost was blocking the only exit.

"Why did you trick us?" Stephanie asked Andrew. "Why did you bring us here? Why did you lie to us?"

Andrew sighed. "I told you. I borrowed this head." He ran one hand through the hair, then down over the cheek, as if petting it. "I borrowed it. But I have to return it."

Stephanie and I stared back at him in silence, waiting for him to continue. Waiting for him to explain.

"I saw you last night in the tour group," he said

finally, his eyes locked on me. "The others couldn't see me. But I made myself visible to you."

"Why?" I asked in a trembling voice.

"Because of your head," he replied. "I liked your head."

"Huh?" A frightened gasp escaped my throat.

He gripped the blond hair again. "I have to return this head, Duane," he said calmly, coldly. "So I'm going to take yours."

27

A frightened giggle escaped my throat.

Why do people suddenly start laughing when they're terrified? I guess it's because if you don't laugh, you'll scream. Or explode or something.

Trapped in that small, dark room with a hundred-year-old ghost that wanted my head, I felt like laughing, screaming, and exploding all at once!

I stared hard at Andrew, squinting in the dim light. "You're kidding, right?"

He shook his head. His silvery eyes narrowed, hard and cold. "I need your head, Duane," he said softly. He shrugged, as if apologizing. "I'll pull it off quickly. It won't hurt a bit."

"But — but I need it, too!" I sputtered.

"I'm only going to borrow it," Andrew said. He took a step toward us. "I'll return it when I find my own head. Promise."

"You're not cheering me up," I replied.

He took another step toward us.

Stephanie and I backed up a step.

He took a step. We backed up a step.

We didn't have much more room to back up. We were nearly to the back wall of pantry shelves.

Suddenly Stephanie spoke up. "Andrew, we'll find your head!" she offered. Her voice shook.

I turned to her. I'd never seen her scared before. Knowing that Stephanie was scared made me *even more* scared!

"For sure!" I croaked. "We'll find your real head. We'll search all night. We know this house really well. I'm sure we can find it if you give us a chance."

He stared back at us without replying.

I wanted to get down on my knees and *beg* him to give us a chance.

But I was afraid that if I got down on my knees, he'd pull off my head.

"We'll find it, Andrew. I *know* we will," Stephanie insisted.

He shook his head. His borrowed head. "There's no way," he murmured sadly. "How long have I been searching this house? For more than a hundred years. For more than a hundred years, I've searched every hallway, every room, every closet."

He took another step closer. His eyes were locked on my head. I knew he was studying it, thinking about how it would look on his shoulders.

"In all these years, I haven't found my head,"

Andrew continued. "So what makes you think you can find it tonight?"

"Well . . . uh . . ." Stephanie turned to me.

"Uh . . . maybe we'll get lucky!" I declared.

Lame. How lame can you get?

"Sorry," Andrew murmured. "I need your head, Duane. We're wasting time."

"Give us a chance!" I cried.

He took a step closer. He was studying my hair now. Probably deciding if he should let it grow longer.

"Andrew — please!" I begged.

It was no use. His eyes were glassy now. He reached out both hands and took another step.

Stephanie and I backed up.

"Give me your head, Duane," the ghost whispered.

My back bumped a shelf on the wall behind me.

"I need your head, Duane."

Stephanie and I huddled close and pressed our backs against the shelves.

The ghost floated closer, hands outstretched.

We pressed ourselves tighter against the shelves. My elbow bumped something hard. I heard some heavy objects fall from the shelf.

"I need your head, Duane."

He clenched and unclenched his hands. Two more steps and he'd be close enough to grab me.

"Your head. Give me your head."

I jammed my back against the shelves.

I heard a creaking sound — and the shelf started to slide.

I stumbled back. And realized that the *whole wall* was sliding.

"Wh-what's happening?" I stammered.

The ghost reached for my head. "Gotcha!"

28

The ghost leaped at me, hands outstretched.

I ducked — and stumbled back as the wall slid away.

The wall made a loud grinding sound as it slowly spun around.

Stephanie fell to the hard floor.

I pulled her up quickly as Andrew made another wild grab for my head.

"A tunnel!" I shouted over the grinding of the wall.

As the wall spun away, it revealed a dark opening. Just big enough to squeeze through.

I pulled Stephanie to the opening — and we squeezed inside.

We found ourselves in a long, low passageway. Some kind of tunnel. Hidden behind the sliding wall.

I'd always heard about old houses that had secret halls and hidden rooms built in them. I never thought I'd be so glad to find one!

Stephanie and I started to run. Our footsteps echoed loudly on the concrete floor.

We ran past bare, concrete walls, cracked and pitted by time. We had to stoop as we ran. The ceiling wasn't as tall as we were!

Stephanie slowed down to glance back. "Is he following us?"

"Just keep running!" I cried. "This tunnel has got to lead out of here! Out of this house! It's *got* to!"

"I can't see *where* it leads!" she replied breathlessly.

The low tunnel stretched out in a straight line. I could see only darkness at the end.

Did it stretch on forever?

If it did, I'd keep running forever. I didn't plan to stop running until I was safely outside.

And once I was outside, I planned never to visit Hill House again. And I planned to stay away from ghosts and to keep my head on my shoulders where it belonged.

Big plans.

But plans don't always work out.

"Ohh!" Stephanie and I both cried out as we nearly crashed into a solid concrete wall.

The tunnel ended. It just ended.

"It — it doesn't go *anywhere*!" I gasped. Breathing hard, I pounded both fists against the wall. "Who would build a secret tunnel that leads nowhere?"

"Push on the wall," Stephanie cried. "Let's both push. Maybe this wall will slide open, too."

We turned and leaned our shoulders into the wall. And pushed. Groaning and gasping, I pushed with all my strength.

I was still pushing when I heard the scraping footsteps moving toward us down the tunnel.

Andrew!

"Push!" Stephanie cried.

We shoved ourselves against the wall.

"Come on — slide! Slide!" I ordered it.

I glanced back and saw Andrew, jogging slowly, steadily toward us.

"We're trapped," Stephanie moaned. She collapsed against the wall with a sigh.

Andrew came trotting closer.

"Duane — I want your head!" he called, his voice echoing against the concrete walls.

"Trapped," Stephanie murmured.

"Maybe not," I choked out. I pointed into the dark corner. "Look. A ladder."

"Huh?" Stephanie leaped to her feet. She squinted at the ladder. A metal ladder, the rungs blanketed with dust. It led straight up the wall, through a small, square opening in the low ceiling.

To where?

"Give me your head!" the ghost called.

I grabbed the sides of the metal ladder. I raised a foot onto the first rung and peered straight up.

Into thick blackness. I couldn't see a thing up there.

"Duane — " Stephanie whispered. "We don't know where it leads!"

"It doesn't matter," I replied, starting to climb. "We don't have a choice — do we?"

29

"Where are you going, Duane? I need your head!"

I ignored the ghost's shout and scrambled up the ladder. Stephanie kept bumping me from behind.

My sneakers slipped on the thick dust. My hands slid over the cold, metal railings.

"Duane — you can't get away!" Andrew called from down below.

Straight up. Straight up the ladder. Stephanie and I, breathing hard, climbing frantically, as fast as we could climb.

Straight up.

Until the ladder started to tilt.

"Noooo!" I uttered a scream as it spilled forward.

A crumbling, cracking noise drowned out my scream.

It took me a few seconds to realize that the wall was breaking apart. Crumbling into powdery chunks.

And we were falling.

I heard Stephanie scream.

I grabbed the metal railings with both hands — and held on tight.

But the ladder was sailing down now. Tumbling over the cracking, crumbling old wall.

"Oww!" I landed hard. Bounced once. Twice.

My hands flew up and I was tossed off the ladder. I rolled onto my stomach, rolled in the chunks of dirt and concrete of the broken wall.

Stephanie landed on her knees. She shook her head, dazed.

Chunks of wall spilled all around us. Stephanie's hair was covered in dust.

I shielded my eyes and waited for the wall to stop crumbling down.

When I opened my eyes, Andrew stood above me. His hands were balled into fists. His mouth hung open. And he was staring . . . staring *past* me.

I struggled to my feet. Turned to see what he was staring at.

"A hidden room!" Stephanie cried, moving beside me. "A room behind the old wall."

Slipping over the chunks of broken concrete, I took a few steps closer to the room.

And saw what Andrew was staring at.

A head.

A boy's head lying on the floor of the hidden room.

"I don't believe it!" Stephanie gasped. "We found it! We actually found it!"

I swallowed hard. And took a careful step forward.

The head was pale, shimmering white, even in the dim light.

I could see clearly that it was a boy's head. But the long, wavy hair had turned to white. The round eyes glowed green, sparkling like emeralds in the shimmering, pale face.

"The ghost head," I murmured.

I turned back to Andrew. "Your head — we found it for you."

I expected to see a smile on his face. I expected him to shout or jump for joy.

For a hundred years, he had waited for this happy moment. And now his long search was over.

But to my shock, Andrew's face was twisted in horror.

He wasn't even looking at his long lost head. He stared above it. And as he stared, his entire body began to quiver. Frightened cries escaped his lips.

"Andrew — what is your problem?" I demanded.

But I don't think he even heard me.

He stared up at the ceiling, trembling. Hands balled into tight fists at his sides. Then, slowly, he raised one hand and pointed. "Nooooo," he moaned. "Ohhhh, nooooooo."

I turned to see what had frightened him.

Turned in time to see a filmy figure float down from the ceiling.

At first I thought it was a thin window curtain, falling from above.

But as it curled slowly, softly to the floor, I saw that it had arms. And legs.

I could see right through it!

The air around us suddenly grew cold.

"It — it's a *ghost*!" Stephanie cried, grabbing my arm.

30

The ghost landed softly, silently on the floor of the hidden room, raising its arms like bird wings.

Stephanie and I both gasped as it raised its arms and stood upright.

It was short and very thin. It wore baggy, old-fashioned-looking pants and a long-sleeved shirt with a high collar.

A high collar.

A collar.

And no head.

The ghost had no head!

I felt a burst of cold air as it bent down, shimmering, bending, as if made of soft gauze. It reached down. Lifted the head off the floor.

Lifted the head to the stiff, tall collar.

Gently pressed the head into place.

And as the head touched the ghostly, gauzy neck, the green eyes flashed.

The cheeks twitched. The pale white eyebrows arched up and down.

And then the mouth moved.

The ghost turned to us — to Stephanie and me. And the lips moved in a silent "Thank you."

"Thank you."

And then the arms rose into the air. Its green eyes still on us, the ghost floated up into the air. Lighter than air, it floated silently up.

I watched in amazement, my heart pounding, until the ghostly figure vanished in the darkness.

And then Stephanie and I both turned to Andrew at the same time. We had just seen the headless ghost. We had just seen Andrew, the boy from a hundred years ago. We had just watched him collect his head.

But the boy who claimed to be Andrew was still there. He stood behind us, still trembling, his eyes wide, staring into the hidden room, making soft swallowing sounds.

I narrowed my eyes at him. "If you aren't Andrew," I started — "if you aren't the headless ghost — then who *are* you?"

31

Stephanie turned on the boy, too. "Yeah. Who are you?" she asked angrily.

"If you're not the headless ghost, why did you chase us?" I demanded.

"Well. I . . . uh . . ." The boy raised both hands as if surrendering. Then he started to back away.

He had only gone three or four steps when we heard footsteps coming down the long tunnel.

I turned to Stephanie. Another ghost?

"Who's in here?" a deep voice boomed.

I saw a circle of light from a flashlight sweeping over the tunnel floor.

"Who is here?" the voice repeated.

I recognized the deep voice. Otto!

"Uh . . . back here," the boy called softly.

"Seth — is that you?" The circle of light floated closer. Otto appeared behind it, squinting at us. "What's going on? What are you doing back here? This part of the house is dangerous. It's all falling apart."

"Well . . . we were exploring," Seth started. "And we got lost. It really wasn't our fault."

Otto gazed at Seth sternly. Then his face filled with surprise as his flashlight washed over Stephanie and me. "You two! How did you get in? What are you doing here?"

"He . . . well . . . he let us in," I answered. I pointed at Seth.

Otto turned back to Seth and shook his head unhappily. "More of your tricks? Were you scaring these kids?"

"Not really, Uncle Otto," Seth replied, keeping his eyes on the ground.

Uncle Otto? So Seth was Otto's nephew!

No wonder he knew so much about Hill House.

"Tell the truth, Seth," Otto insisted. "Were you pretending to be a ghost again? Haven't you played that trick on enough kids? Haven't you scared enough kids to death?"

Seth stood silent.

Otto rubbed a hand back over his smooth, bald head. Then he let out a weary sigh. "We have a business to run here," he told Seth. "Do you want to scare my customers away? Do you want to get the whole neighborhood upset?"

Seth lowered his head and still didn't reply.

I could see that he was in major trouble. So I decided to jump in. "It's okay, Otto," I said. "He didn't scare us."

"That's right," Stephanie chimed in. "We didn't believe he was a ghost. Did we, Duane?"

"Of course not," I replied. "He didn't fool us for a minute."

"Especially when we saw the *real* ghost," Stephanie added.

Otto turned to her, studying her in the light from the flashlight. "The *what*?"

"The real ghost!" Stephanie insisted.

"We saw the real ghost, Uncle Otto!" Seth exclaimed. "It was *awesome*!"

Otto rolled his eyes. "Save the jokes, Seth. It's too late at night. You're just trying to get out of trouble."

"No. Really!" I insisted.

"Really!" Seth and Stephanie cried.

"We saw the headless ghost, Uncle Otto. You've got to believe us!" Seth pleaded.

"Sure, sure," Otto muttered. He turned and motioned with his flashlight. "Come on. Everyone out."

32

After our scary night at Hill House, Stephanie and I gave up haunting the neighborhood.

It just wasn't that exciting anymore. Especially since we'd seen a real ghost.

We stopped sneaking out at night. We stopped peeking into kids' windows in scary masks. We stopped hiding behind bushes and howling like werewolves in the middle of the night.

We gave up all the scary stuff. And we never even talked about ghosts.

Stephanie and I found other things to be interested in. I tried out for the basketball team at school, and I became a starting forward.

Stephanie joined the Theater Arts Club. This spring, she's going to be Dorothy in *The Wizard of Oz*. Either Dorothy or a Munchkin.

We had a good winter. Lots of snow. Lots of unscary fun.

Then late one evening we were heading home from a birthday party. It was the first warm night of spring. Tulips were blooming in some of the front yards we passed. The air smelled fresh and sweet.

I stopped in front of Hill House and gazed up at the old mansion. Stephanie stopped beside me. She read my mind. "You want to go in, don't you, Duane?"

I nodded. "How about taking the tour? We haven't been in there since . . ." My voice trailed off.

"Hey, why not?" Stephanie replied.

We climbed the steep hill. Tall weeds brushed the legs of my jeans as I made my way to the front door. The huge old house stood as dark and as creepy as ever.

As Stephanie and I climbed onto the front stoop, the door creaked open. As it always had.

We stepped into the small front entryway. A few seconds later, Otto bounced into view. Dressed all in black. A friendly smile on his round, bald head.

"You two!" he exclaimed happily. "Welcome back." He called into the front room. "Edna, come see who is here."

Edna came tottering into the room. "Oh, my!" she cried, pressing a hand against her pale, wrinkled face. "We were wondering if we would see you two again."

I gazed into the front room. No other customers.

"Could you take us on the tour?" I asked Otto.

He smiled his toothy smile. "Of course. Wait. I'll get my lantern."

Otto took us around Hill House. He gave us the complete tour.

It was great to see the house again. But it no longer held any secrets for Stephanie and me.

After the tour, we thanked Otto and said good night.

We were halfway down the hill when a police car pulled up to the curb. A dark-uniformed officer stuck his head out of the passenger window. "What were you kids doing up there?" he called.

Stephanie and I made our way down to the police car. The two officers eyed us suspiciously.

"We just took the tour," I explained, pointing up to Hill House.

"Tour? What tour?" the officer demanded gruffly.

"You know. The haunted house tour," Stephanie replied impatiently.

The police officer stuck his head farther out the window. He had blue eyes, and freckles all over his face. "What were you *really* doing up there?" he asked softly.

"We *told* you," I said shrilly. "Taking the tour. That's all."

Behind the wheel, the other policeman chuckled. "Maybe a ghost gave them the tour," he told his partner.

112

"There *are* no tours," the freckle-faced officer said, frowning. "There haven't been any tours in that house for months."

Stephanie and I both uttered cries of surprise.

"The house is empty," the police officer continued. "Shut down. There hasn't been anyone in there all winter. Hill House went out of business three months ago."

"Huh?" Stephanie and I exchanged startled glances. Then we both turned to gaze up at the house.

The gray stone turrets rose up into the purple-black sky. Nothing but darkness all around.

And then I saw a trail of soft light across the front window. Lantern light. Orange and soft as smoke.

In the soft light, I saw Otto and Edna. They floated in front of the window. I could see right through them, as if they were made of gauze.

They're ghosts, too, I realized, staring into the soft, smoky light.

I blinked. And the light faded out.

Add *more*

Goosebumps®

to your collection . . .

Here's a chilling preview of

MONSTER BLOOD II

2

"Don't bury me. *Please* don't bury me!" Evan murmured.

He heard laughter.

He raised his head and glanced around — and realized that he wasn't home in his back yard. He was sitting in his assigned seat in the third row near the window in Mr. Murphy's science class.

And Mr. Murphy was standing right at Evan's side, his enormous, round body blocking the sunlight from the window. "Earth calling Evan! Earth calling Evan!" Mr. Murphy called, cupping his chubby pink hands over his mouth to make a megaphone.

The kids all laughed.

Evan could feel his face growing hot. "S-sorry," he stammered.

"You seem to have been somewhere in Daydream Land," Mr. Murphy said, his tiny black eyes twinkling merrily.

"Yes," Evan replied solemnly. "I was dreaming about Monster Blood. I — I can't stop thinking about it."

Ever since his frightening adventure the past summer with the green, sticky stuff, Evan had been dreaming and daydreaming about it.

"Evan, please," Mr. Murphy said softly. He shook his round, pink head and made a "tsk-tsk" sound.

"Monster Blood is real!" Evan blurted out angrily.

The kids laughed again.

Mr. Murphy's expression grew stern. His tiny eyes locked onto Evan's. "Evan, I am a science teacher. You don't expect a science teacher to believe that you found a can of sticky green gunk in a toy store that makes things grow and grow."

"Y-yes, I do," Evan insisted.

"Maybe a science-*fiction* teacher would believe it," Mr. Murphy replied, grinning at his own joke. "Not a *science* teacher."

"Well, you're dumb!" Evan cried.

He didn't mean to say it. He knew immediately that he had just made a major mistake.

He heard gasps all around the big classroom.

Mr. Murphy's pink face darkened until it looked like a red balloon. But he didn't lose his temper. He clasped his chubby hands over the big stomach of his green sportshirt, and Evan could see him silently counting to ten.

"Evan, you're a new student here, isn't that right?" he asked finally. His face slowly returned to its normal pink color.

"Yes," Evan replied, his voice just above a whisper. "My family just moved to Atlanta this fall."

"Well, perhaps you're not familiar with the way things work here. Perhaps at your old school the teachers liked it when you called them dumb. Perhaps you called your teachers ugly names all day long. Perhaps —"

"No, sir," Evan interrupted, lowering his head. "It just slipped out."

Laughter rang through the classroom. Mr. Murphy glared sternly at Evan, his face twisted in an angry frown.

Give me a break, Evan thought unhappily. Glancing quickly around the room, Evan saw a sea of grinning faces.

I think I'm in trouble again, Evan thought glumly. Why can't I keep my big mouth shut?

Mr. Murphy glanced up at the wall clock. "School is nearly over," he said. "Why don't you do us all a little favor, Evan, to make up for the time you made us waste today?"

Uh oh, Evan thought darkly. Here it comes.

"When the bell rings, go put your books away in

your locker," Mr. Murphy instructed. "Then come back here and clean Cuddles's cage."

Evan groaned.

His eyes darted to the hamster cage against the wall. Cuddles was scratching around in the wood shavings on the cage floor.

Not the hamster! Evan thought unhappily.

Evan hated Cuddles. And Mr. Murphy knew it. This was the third time Mr. Murphy had made Evan stay after school and clean out the gross, disgusting cage.

"Perhaps while you clean the hamster cage," Mr. Murphy said, returning to his desk, "you can think about how to do better in science class, Evan."

Evan jumped to his feet. "I won't do it!" he cried.

He heard shocked gasps all around him.

"I hate Cuddles!" Evan screamed. "I *hate* that stupid, fat hamster!"

As everyone stared in amazed horror, Evan ran over to the cage, pulled open the door, and grabbed Cuddles up in one hand.

Then, with an easy, graceful motion, he flung the hamster across the room — and out the open window.

3

Evan knew he was having another daydream.

He didn't jump up screaming and throw the hamster out the window.

He only thought about it. *Everyone* thinks about doing crazy, wild things once in a while.

But Evan would never do anything that crazy.

Instead, he said, "Okay, Mr. Murphy." Then he sat quietly in his seat, staring out the window at the puffy white clouds in the bright blue sky.

He could see his own reflection staring back at him in the glass. His curly, carrot-colored hair looked darker in the reflection. So did the freckles that dotted his cheeks.

His expression was mournful. He hated being made fun of in front of the entire class.

Why am I always getting myself into trouble? he wondered. Why can't Mr. Murphy ever give me a break? Didn't the teacher realize how hard it was to be the new kid in school? How am I supposed to make new friends if Murphy is always making me look like a total jerk in class?

Bad enough that no one believed him about the Monster Blood.

Evan had eagerly told the kids in his new school about it. How he had stayed with his great-aunt the past summer. How he and a girl he met named Andy had found the blue container of Monster Blood in a creepy, old toy store.

And how the green, yucky Monster Blood had started to grow and grow. How it had bubbled out of its container, outgrown a bucket, outgrown a *bath tub*! And just kept growing and growing as if it were alive!

And Evan had told kids how Trigger had eaten just a little of the Monster Blood — and had grown nearly as big as a house!

It was such a frightening, amazing story. Evan was sure his new friends would find it really cool.

But, instead, they just thought he was weird.

No one believed him. They laughed at him and told him he had a sick imagination.

Evan became known around his new school as the kid who made up stupid stories.

If only I could prove to them that the story is true, Evan often thought sadly. If only I could show them the Monster Blood.

But the mysterious green gunk had vanished

from sight before Evan left his great-aunt's house. Not a trace of it had been left. Not a trace.

The bell rang. Everyone jumped up and headed for the door, talking and laughing.

Evan knew that a lot of his classmates were laughing at *him*. Ignoring them, Evan picked up his backpack and started to the door.

"Hurry back, Evan," Mr. Murphy called from behind his desk. "Cuddles is waiting!"

Evan growled under his breath and stepped out into the crowded hallway. If Murphy loves that stupid hamster so much, why doesn't *he* ever clean out the cage? he wondered bitterly.

A group of kids laughed loudly as Evan passed by. Were they laughing at him? Evan couldn't tell.

He started jogging to his locker — when something hit his leg just above the ankle. His feet flew out from under him, and he toppled face down onto the hard tile floor.

"Hey — !" Evan cried angrily.

He stared up at a big, tough-looking kid from his class named Conan Barber. All the kids called him Conan the Barbarian. For good reason.

Conan was twelve, but he looked about twenty years older! He was taller and wider and stronger and meaner than any kid in the school.

He wasn't a bad-looking guy, Evan grudgingly admitted. He had wavy, blond hair, blue eyes, and a handsome face. He was very athletic-looking, and played all the sports at school.

He was an okay guy, Evan thought wistfully. Except that he had one very bad habit. Conan loved to live up to his nickname.

He *loved* being Conan the Barbarian.

He loved strutting around, pounding kids who weren't his size — which included *everyone*!

Evan had not hit it off with Conan.

He met Conan on the playground a few weeks after moving to Atlanta. Eager to make a good impression, Evan told him the whole Monster Blood story.

Conan didn't like the story. He stared back at Evan with his cold, blue eyes for a long, long time. Then his expression hardened, and he murmured through clenched teeth: "We don't like wise guys down here in Atlanta."

He gave Evan a pretty good pounding that day.

Evan had tried to stay away from Conan ever since. But it wasn't easy.

Now he gazed up at Conan from his position on the floor. "Hey — why'd you trip me?" Evan demanded shrilly.

Conan grinned down at him and shrugged. "It was an accident."

Evan tried to decide whether it was safer to stand up or to stay down on the floor. If I stand up, he'll punch me, he thought. If I stay down here, he'll step on me.

Tough choice.

He didn't get to make it. Conan reached down and, with one hand, pulled Evan to his feet.

"Give me a break, Conan!" Evan pleaded. "Why can't you leave me alone?"

Conan shrugged again. It was one of his favorite replies. His blue eyes twinkled merrily. "You're right, Evan," he said, his grin fading. "I shouldn't have tripped you."

"Yeah," Evan agreed, straightening his T-shirt.

"So you can pay me back," Conan offered.

"Huh?" Evan gaped at him.

Conan stuck out his massive chest. "Go ahead. Hit me in the stomach. I'll let you."

"Whoa. No way," Evan replied, trying to back up. He stumbled into a group of kids.

"Go ahead," Conan urged, following after him. "Hit me in the stomach. As hard as you can. It's only fair."

Evan studied his expression. "You really mean it?"

Conan nodded, tight-lipped. He stuck out his chest. "As hard as you can. Go ahead. I won't hit back. I promise."

Evan hesitated. Should he go ahead and do it?

I may never get a chance like this again, he thought.

A lot of kids were watching, Evan realized.

If I hit him really hard, if I hurt him, if I make him cry out — then maybe kids around here will have a little respect for me.

I'll be Evan the Giant Killer. The guy who pounded Conan the Barbarian.

He balled his hand into a tight fist and raised it.

"Is *that* your fist?" Conan cried, laughing.

Evan nodded.

"Oooh — this is going to hurt!" Conan cried sarcastically. He made his knees tremble.

Everyone laughed.

I may surprise him, Evan thought angrily.

"Go ahead. As hard as you can," Conan urged. He sucked in a deep breath and held it.

Evan pulled his arm back and swung his fist as hard as he could.

The fist made a solid *thud* as it hit Conan's stomach.

It felt like hitting a concrete wall.

Evan's hand throbbed with pain.

"Hey — !" a man's voice called angrily.

Startled, Evan spun around — to see Mr. Murphy glaring at him.

"No fighting!" Mr. Murphy yelled at Evan.

The teacher came bouncing up to them and stepped between the two boys. Huffing for breath, he turned to Conan. "Why did Evan hit you?" he demanded.

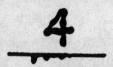

Conan shrugged. His blue eyes went wide and innocent. "I don't know, Mr. Murphy," he replied in a tiny, forlorn voice. "Evan just walked up and hit me as hard as he could."

Conan rubbed his stomach and uttered a short whimper. "Ow. He really hurt me."

Mr. Murphy narrowed his beady black eyes at Evan. His chubby face turned bright red again. "Evan, I saw the whole thing. I really don't understand you," he said softly.

"But Mr. Murphy — " Evan started.

The teacher raised a hand to silence him. "If you were angry about what happened in class," Mr. Murphy said, "you shouldn't take it out on other kids."

Conan rubbed his stomach tenderly. "I hope Evan didn't *break* anything!" he murmured.

"Do you want to see the nurse?" Mr. Murphy asked.

Conan shook his head. Evan could see he was having trouble keeping a straight face. "I'll be okay," he said, and staggered away.

What a phony! Evan thought bitterly.

Did Conan know the whole time that Murphy was standing there? Probably.

"Go take care of Cuddles," Mr. Murphy told Evan, frowning. "And try to shape up, Evan. I'm going to be watching you."

Evan muttered a reply and trudged back into the classroom. Sunlight streamed in through the wall of windows. A strong breeze made the window shade flap over the open window near the teacher's desk.

Feeling angry and upset, his stomach churning, Evan made his way through the empty room to the hamster cage. Cuddles wrinkled his nose in greeting. The hamster knew the routine by now.

Evan gazed into the metal cage at the brown-and-white creature. Why do people think hamsters are cute? he wondered.

Because they wrinkle their noses? Because they run around and around on wheels like total jerks? Because of their cute little buck teeth?

Cuddles stared up at him with his little black eyes.

He has Mr. Murphy's eyes, Evan thought, chuckling to himself. Maybe that's why Murphy likes him so much.

"Okay, okay. So you're kind of cute," Evan told the hamster. "But I know your secret. You're just a big fat rat in disguise!"

Cuddles wrinkled his nose again in reply.

With a loud sigh, Evan went to work. Holding his breath because he hated the smell, he pulled out the bottom tray.

"You're a messy little guy," he told the hamster. "When are you going to learn to clean up your own room?"

Still holding his breath, he dumped out the old newspaper shavings and replaced them with fresh shavings from the box in the supply closet.

He returned the bottom tray to its place as Cuddles watched with great interest. Then he poured fresh water into the water bottle.

"How about some sunflower seeds?" Evan asked. He began to feel a little more cheerful, knowing his job was almost finished.

He removed the seed cup from the cage and made his way across the room to the supply closet to get fresh sunflower seeds.

"Okay, Cuddles," he called, "these look yummy!"

He started to carry the seeds back to the cage. Halfway across the room, Evan stopped and uttered a startled gasp.

The cage door hung wide open.

The hamster was gone.

5

A choking sound escaped Evan's lips as he stared at the empty cage.

His eyes darted frantically around the room. "Cuddles? Cuddles?" he called in a frightened voice.

Why am I yelling? he asked himself, spinning around in a total panic. The dumb hamster doesn't know its name!

He heard footsteps out in the hall.

Mr. Murphy?

No, please — no! Evan pleaded silently.

Don't let it be Mr. Murphy. Don't let him return until I have Cuddles safely back in his cage.

Cuddles was Mr. Murphy's most precious possession. He had told this to the class time and again.

Evan knew that if anything happened to Cuddles, Mr. Murphy would be on Evan's case for the rest of the year. No — for the rest of his *life*!

Evan froze in the center of the room, listening hard.

The footsteps passed by the room.

Evan started breathing again.

"Cuddles? Where are you, Cuddles?" he called in a trembling voice. "I have some delicious sunflower seeds for you."

He spotted the furry, brown-and-white creature on the chalk tray under the front chalkboard.

"There you are! I see you!" Evan whispered, tiptoeing toward it.

Cuddles was busily chewing on something. A small piece of white chalk.

Evan tiptoed closer. "I have seeds for you, Cuddles," he whispered. "Much tastier than chalk."

Cuddles held the stick of chalk in his front paws, turning it as he chewed.

Evan crept closer. Closer.

"Look. Seeds." He held the plastic seed cup toward the hamster.

Cuddles didn't look up.

Evan crept up closer. Closer.

Close enough to dive forward —

— and *miss*!

The hamster dropped the chalk and scampered down the chalk tray.

Evan made another frantic grab — and came up with nothing but air.

Letting out a frustrated groan, Evan saw the hamster dive to the floor and scamper behind Mr. Murphy's desk. The hamster's feet skidded and slid on the linoleum floor, its toenails clicking loudly.

"You can't get away! You're too fat!" Evan cried. He dropped to his knees and peered under the desk.

He could see Cuddles staring back at him from the darkness. The animal was breathing rapidly, its sides swelling with each breath.

"Don't be scared," Evan whispered soothingly. "I'm going to put you back in your nice, safe cage."

He crawled quickly to the desk.

The hamster stared back at him, breathing hard. It didn't move — until Evan reached for him. Then Cuddles scampered away, his tiny paws sliding on the floor.

Evan jumped angrily to his feet. "Cuddles — what's your problem?" he demanded loudly. "This isn't a stupid game!"

It wasn't a game at all, Evan knew.

If he didn't get the hamster back in the cage, Mr. Murphy would flunk him for sure. Or suspend him from school. Or get his family kicked out of Atlanta!

Calm down, Evan urged himself. Don't panic.

He took a deep breath and held it.

Then he saw the hamster on the window ledge just inside the open window.

Okay, Evan — go ahead and panic! he told himself.

This was definitely panic time.

He tried to call to the hamster. But his voice came out a choked whisper.

Swallowing hard, Evan edged slowly toward the window ledge.

"Come here, Cuddles," he whispered. "Please, Cuddles — come here."

Closer, closer.

Almost close enough to reach the hamster.

Almost close enough.

"Don't move, Cuddles. Don't move."

He reached out his hand slowly. Slowly.

Cuddles glanced back at him with his soft black eyes.

Then the hamster jumped out the window.

About the Author

R.L. STINE is the author of the series *Fear Street*, *Nightmare Room*, *Give Yourself Goosebumps*, and the phenomenally successful *Goosebumps*. His thrilling teen titles have sold more than 250 million copies internationally — enough to earn him a spot in the *Guinness Book of World Records*! Mr. Stine lives in New York City with his wife, Jane, and his son, Matt.

YOU'VE READ THE BOOKS...
NOW OWN THE THRILLS ON DVD

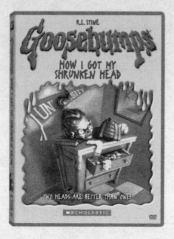

BRING HOME
THE EXCITEMENT!

R.L. Stine Classics
Come To DVD
For The First Time
From Twentieth Century
Fox Home Entertainment!

www.foxhome.com

SCHOLASTIC

www.scholastic.com/

Collect Them All!

Goosebumps®

By R.L. Stine

Each Book $4.99

- ❏ Goosebumps: Abominable Snowman of Pasadena
- ❏ Goosebumps: Attack of the Jack-O-Lanterns
- ❏ Goosebumps: Attack of The Mutant
- ❏ Goosebumps: Bad Hare Day
- ❏ Goosebumps: Barking Ghost
- ❏ Goosebumps: The Beast from the East
- ❏ Goosebumps: Be Careful What You Wish For...
- ❏ Goosebumps: The Cuckoo Clock of Doom
- ❏ Goosebumps: The Curse of Camp Cold Lake
- ❏ Goosebumps: Curse of the Mummy's Tomb
- ❏ Goosebumps: Deep Trouble
- ❏ Goosebumps: Egg Monsters from Mars
- ❏ Goosebumps: Ghost Beach
- ❏ Goosebumps: Ghost Camp
- ❏ Goosebumps: Ghost Next Door
- ❏ Goosebumps: The Girl Who Cried Monster
- ❏ Goosebumps: Go Eat Worms!
- ❏ Goosebumps: The Haunted Mask
- ❏ Goosebumps: The Haunted Mask II
- ❏ Goosebumps: The Headless Ghost
- ❏ Goosebumps: The Horror at Camp Jellyjam
- ❏ Goosebumps: How I Got My Shrunken Head
- ❏ Goosebumps: How to Kill a Monster
- ❏ Goosebumps: It Came from Beneath the Sink!
- ❏ Goosebumps: Lets Get Invisible
- ❏ Goosebumps: Monster Blood
- ❏ Goosebumps: Monster Blood II
- ❏ Goosebumps: A Night in Terror Tower
- ❏ Goosebumps: Night of the Living Dummy
- ❏ Goosebumps: Night of the Living Dummy II
- ❏ Goosebumps: Night of the Living Dummy III
- ❏ Goosebumps: One Day at HorrorLand
- ❏ Goosebumps: Piano Lessons Can Be Murder
- ❏ Goosebumps: Revenge of the Lawn Gnomes
- ❏ Goosebumps: Say Cheese and Die!
- ❏ Goosebumps: Say Cheese and Die — Again!
- ❏ Goosebumps: The Scarecrow Walks at Midnight
- ❏ Goosebumps: Shocker on Shock Street
- ❏ Goosebumps: Stay Out of the Basement
- ❏ Goosebumps: Vampire Breath
- ❏ Goosebumps: Welcome to Camp Nightmare
- ❏ Goosebumps: Welcome to Dead House
- ❏ Goosebumps: The Werewolf of Fever Swamp
- ❏ Goosebumps: Why I'm Afraid of Bees
- ❏ Goosebumps: You Can't Scare Me!

■SCHOLASTIC

GBKLST0805

Read at Your Own Risk

Goosebumps

By R. L. Stine

Each Book $4.99

____ 0-439-72705-8 Goosebumps: Attack of the Jack-O-Lanterns

____ 0-439-66215-X Goosebumps: Attack of The Mutant

____ 0-439-66216-8 Goosebumps: Bad Hare Day

____ 0-439-66990-1 Goosebumps: Be Careful What You Wish For

____ 0-439-72403-1 Goosebumps: The Beast from the East

____ 0-439-72404-X Goosebumps: The Curse of Camp Cold Lake

____ 0-439-56828-5 Goosebumps: Deep Trouble

____ 0-439-56829-3 Goosebumps: Egg Monsters from Mars

____ 0-439-56830-7 Goosebumps: Ghost Beach

____ 0-439-56831-5 Goosebumps: Ghost Camp

____ 0-439-69353-5 Goosebumps: The Girl Who Cried Monster

____ 0-439-67114-0 Goosebumps: Go Eat Worms!

____ 0-439-67113-2 Goosebumps: The Haunted Mask II

____ 0-439-66987-1 Goosebumps: The Headless Ghost

____ 0-439-56837-4 Goosebumps: It Came from Beneath the Sink!

____ 0-439-66988-X Goosebumps: Monster Blood II

____ 0-439-67111-6 Goosebumps: A Night in Terror Tower

____ 0-439-57374-2 Goosebumps: Night of the Living Dummy II

____ 0-439-66989-8 Goosebumps: Night of the Living Dummy III

____ 0-439-56841-2 Goosebumps: One Day at HorrorLand

____ 0-439-67112-4 Goosebumps: Piano Lessons Can Be Murder

____ 0-439-57375-0 Goosebumps: Revenge of the Lawn Gnomes

____ 0-439-56842-0 Goosebumps: Say Cheese and Die!

____ 0-439-57361-0 Goosebumps: Say Cheese and Die—Again!

____ 0-439-56843-9 Goosebumps: The Scarecrow Walks at Midnight

____ 0-439-72706-6 Goosebumps: Vampire Breath

____ 0-439-56846-3 Goosebumps: Welcome to Camp Nightmare

____ 0-439-56848-X Goosebumps: The Werewolf of Fever Swamp

____ 0-439-57365-3 Goosebumps: You Can't Scare Me!

____ 0-439-69354-3 Goosebumps: Why Im Afraid of Bees

Available Wherever Books Are Sold, or Use This Order Form.

■SCHOLASTIC